RDANT
SLAND S

AN

ÆLFWYNN
VILLAGE

PAKARR
VILLAGE

SLUMBERING WOODS

UNITED VEL
PROVINCE

CHAUNT RIVER

CALACK
CITY

MONDE
DESSERT

DANCAR
MOUNTAINS

SHADOW
CITY

DARK
CASTLE

OCEAN

300 ML

The Day it Started

The day it all started was a normal one for Tala. "Tala what did I just say the answer to question number 4 was?" "um, was it manifest destiny" said Tala hoping the response would not be a detention. "No" said Ms. Clark "maybe if you spent more time paying attention and less time day dreaming you would know the answer don't let me catch you doing it again." "Yes Ms. Clark" said Tala. "what a witch" thought Tala like any one would care about stupid old settlers the cool history was all about tombs and sword fights, ancient myths, and kings now that was cool she sighed and tried to look like she was listening Tala was tired of pretending to care, she had always felt that way like she was out of place. So she threw herself into fantasy hoping one day she would get into a real adventure .The truth was Tala really was nothing special she had just turned sixteen and she was not very smart nor was she pretty or athletic. Her name was unique but it only worked against her. Tapping her pencil on the desk she thought about what to do the coming weekend. It was Friday and history was her last period class she had nothing to look forward to the boys at her school didn't get her and the girls were even worse. So dating and sleep overs were not in the cards for her and yet she couldn't wait to be free of the torment that was school. Suddenly the final bell rang and she hurried home. She got a ride with her only friend Sarah they got along but rarely hung out outside of school Tala didn't really share her interests . When they got to Tala's house Sarah asked if she wanted to try and crash this party she heard was going on the next day even though neither of them had been invited. Tala politely turned her down with some lame excuse and ran into the house. It was a nice place her dad did okay for them he was a lawyer it was a good job but it was stressful and he worked long hours so it did get lonely. It was just the two of them Tala's mother had died when she was two. Tala did not remember her but she did have pictures her mother was beautiful blond hair and a face that drew everyone in a room to her nothing like herself. No Tala looked more like her father tall with messy black hair a small nose and distant gray eyes. When she got home she started dinner. Cooking was one of her better skills she had been doing it almost her whole life. After she had gotten it started she curled up on the coach and finished a particularity good book she had been reading filled with magic and danger and wished that her life was like the heroes in the book. She thought more about what it would be like and even darted around the room a little, sparing imaginary swordsmen. The sound of her father closing the front door jarred her out of her fantasy and she rushed out to greet him giving him a big kiss and said "I started dinner" it will be ready in a half hour. "Oh Tala you shouldn't have I could have made something." "Yes but I thought it would be better if it weren't burnt" said Tala. "Oww! That was a low blow" said her father and they both laughed. "How was your day" Tala asked "long" said her father "we lost the Stevens case and …Oh I'd rather not talk about work". Tala's father worked for the district attorney. Ted Stevens was a high profile drug dealer and apparently he was going free she understood why he didn't want to talk about it. "So how was your day?" "boring" said Tala "as usual." "You get used to it" said her father pausing he said "what's that smell?" "oh no the potatoes" yelled Tala and ran in to the kitchen. "So much for it not being burnt" laughed her father.

After dinner Tala lay in her bed thinking as she often did with her free time, this time she was thinking about writing a book. Her mother had been an author and Tala thought it might be nice to follow in her footsteps. She thought and thought and had come up with the idea for the hero a wizard named Aden and a villain who's name she was trying to come up with as she drifted slowly to sleep. That night Tala dreamt of a magical land where her dreams came true and she fought with a sword in hand to defeat the evil of the land.

****

Aden awoke with a start, filled with terror, relaxing when he realized where he was, another nightmare he thought. They had tormented him often of late "at least its morning." He mused over going back to sleep but ultimately decided to get up "I've got work to do" he said to himself. He got out of bed and got dressed buckling his belt and attaching his sheathed sword . After buttoning his cloak he flipped back the hood to reveal a head full of red spiky hair. It should have looked unnatural but on him it seemed as mundane as having white teeth. Finally he attached his bracers now fully dressed he pulled a small sack from his waist and produced a pinch of ash from it which he placed on his shoulder. Then he yelled "braaand!, Brand come on" to the open air silence was his only answer. Then slowly a small flame burst from the ash on his shoulder and grew twisting and bending its shape until it was about half a foot in diameter and then formed the shape of large flaming bird that most closely resembled a bright red falcon. "Ah! There you are" said Aden feeding the bird a piece of charcoal. "let's get going then" finally he placed the bag that held all his medallions scrolls and other artifacts commonly carried by a wizard and left the room at the inn he had been staying at for the last week.

He descended the stairs to the first floor of the inn. The innkeeper yelled at him as he exited the stairs. "I thought I told you not to summon that disaster waiting to happen inside my inn" said Rohan the innkeeper. "Brand would never be so clumsy as to set the inn on fire. Besides I'm leaving now I left the money for my stay on the bed in my room thanks for everything Rohan." "But you just got back home are you sure you want to leave so soon" said Rohan. "Yes it looks like no one's knows more about him than I do and I shouldn't linger here. Pakarr village hasn't been my home since I left I can't return here until I've found Raven." "You can't blame yourself for what happened" said Rohan "now stop this foolishness and move back home." "Goodbye Rohan" said Aden with a smile and he left. By the time he had closed the door behind him the smile had left his face replaced by a sad frown and a look of determination. With a sigh he turned and started walking, and did not look back once .After a long day of travel Aden stopped in a clearing of the dense forest brand and he had been traveling though and said "well brand we better camp here we won't reach the Chaunt river till tomorrow." *"Are you sure"* said brand in a flickering voice similar to that of his fiery complexion. *"It's a full moon to night the werewolves are sure to be out."* "Like I'm afraid" said Aden "I don't care If it's a hundred wolves I'll take 'em all on and win without breaking a sweat." Brand chose not to respond, for all the bad things that had happened to Aden he was still the loudmouth knuckle head he had always been getting into fights too big for him. Brand on the other hand was much calmer saying little even to Aden. Brand had often wondered why he had been chosen as Aden's familiar and had decided the gods must know something he didn't. Aden was not surprised when brand didn't answer, and instead flew into a nearby tree to sleep, Aden was a fire wizard but that was not all he could do. Removing a tarp from his pack he placed it under the tree brand was roosting in and concentrated. After a few moments the tarp came to life molded itself into a tent and froze rigid. The display of morphing magic took more out of him than fire magic did and when he lied down in the tent he fell asleep almost instantly.

Aden awoke to the sounds of screaming and inhuman growling. He wasted no time jumping up and running to the aid of whoever needed it and without having to say anything brand joined him in racing to investigate the noise. After running for a minute or two though the trees Aden entered a clearing and froze there standing in the middle of the clearing was the most beautiful woman he had ever seen surrounded by 7 of the largest meanest looking werewolves he had ever seen.

****

Tala awoke in a cold mysterious place deeply confused she looked around but her confusion only deepened. She was lying on the ground in the middle of a strange dark forest, but that wasn't all she felt strange like her body wasn't hers. Disoriented she sat up looked at herself and gasped.

She was dressed in beautiful white clothing that turned into leggings at the waist except the back which went to the ground like a cloak the dress was complete with a hood and a belt made of pure silver on which hung a sword in a sheath.

When she clutched her head in surprise she was even more surprised to find she had pointed ears, slanted eyes and other catlike features. "What, what has happened to me, what's going on, is this a dream" she said out loud for no one to hear "where am I what is this!" It couldn't be a dream it was so real. She crawled to a nearby puddle and looked at her reflection "I'm green!" she said shocked "and beautiful?" Tala was amazed by how pretty she appeared after her strange transformation. It was so alien and yet familiar her new look reminded her of her mother. Suddenly even considering the amazing situation she was in she couldn't help but think of the mother she had lost and the time together that they never had. She began to think of what her mother might have been like when she was alive when she heard a branch snap, that Tala wouldn't have heard without her new foreign senses. on a reflex that wasn't her own she leap 10 feet backward in a show of inhuman flexibility agility and power, just as a giant hairy monster leaped bursting though the nearby tree line and landed upon the spot she was just sitting with a crash leaving a small crater in the ground. Without pause it turned and charged her again she leaped out of the way just in time. "I can't be doing this" Tala thought "this can't be happening I must be dreaming". She dodged the monster several more times and landed in the middle of the clearing breathing hard and watching the monster, it had paused in its assault and was staring at her, it almost appeared to be smiling, then she smelled their hot moist breath smelling of rotting meat and realized she was surrounded.

  Aden wasn't sure what to do. Werewolves were impervious to most magic and no swordsman no matter how good stood a chance against seven of them. *Leave her said brand she's doomed don't sacrifice yourself in vain.* Aden stood there for a moment thinking then spoke "I have to try." He drew his sword and ran at the nearest wolf *foolish human* brand said and flew after him the wolf turned to him and would have killed him had brand not flown into the monsters face temporarily blinding it Aden took the opportunity and drove his blade though the heart of the wolf killing it. Seeing this three of the wolves broke from the main pack an engaged Aden the one on the left took a swing at him and he deflected the claws with his sword it staggered and he stabbed at the wolf but he missed its heart. Before he could strike again a second wolf charged at him brand flew at the beast but it was ready and batted him to the ground, and his flames burned out as he died leaving behind a pile of ash. Seeing brand killed Aden roared with anger and with one stroke separated the beasts head from its body. He cried in triumph but his cry was stifled as he was forced to duck another swing from a werewolf, after a series of dodges and parry's it slowly occurred to Aden he could not defeat the two remaining wolves by himself.

Tala was horrified she saw what was happening to the man that came to help her but she could not help him any more than she could help herself. She fell to the ground hopeless as three wolves closed on her in sheer panic she beat the ground yelling. "I want it to stop I just want it to stop." Then as she was pounding the ground and just as the wolves were about to pounce on them both the ground shook with such a ferocity that Aden fell to his knees just as a werewolf was about to behead him and the werewolves around Tala where knocked off balance. The ground continued to shake, and then slowly from the ground beside Tala a giant man made from plants, dirt, and stone blended perfectly together rose from the ground.

The giant artificial being dragged itself from the ground and stood for a moment its presence dominating the clearing. Everything in the clearing froze waiting to see what it would do. It wasted no time showing them with one strike the being smashed the closest wolf to paste. Turning their attentions away from Tala the two remaining wolves jumped onto the behemoth and bit and tore at the being but they were clearly doing no damage. It hardly seemed to notice the attack as it threw one wolf a hundred yards into the nearby treetops, and then turned toward the last wolf it grabbed the beast by the jaws and tore the animal in two with its giant arms causing a sickening ripping sound. The giant man gave Aden just the advantage he needed he easily dispatched a nearby now entirely distracted werewolf and turned to the last wolf. He was confident he could win in a one to one fight. He charged at the beast which roared in anger and was preparing to charge when it suddenly froze.

The first rays of sunlit crept over the landscape and illuminated Aden's foe, no longer a werewolf but a girl no older than 10 stood before him. She stared at him with an intense gaze and Aden did not know what to do. She had only time to say "where are they" in a sleepy voice then she stumbled towards him and collapsed. Aden dropped his sword and caught the girl before she hit the ground. "I guess it is a lucky night for this one, if a werewolf ever had a lucky full moon.

Tala unfurled from the frightened ball she had rolled into during the Golem's rampage when she realized all the monsters that had attacked her were dead. Before her stood the monster that she should be even more afraid of but something deep inside her told her it would not harm her. The giant man covered in fresh blood and made of sticks and leaves, forearms made from tree trunks and fists made of stone would have scared anyone else half to death but not her, instead she thanked the beast.

Then the giant man nodded and slowly sunk back into the ground. Tala turned to thank her other hero and saw him catch a little girl in a tattered dress as she passed out. Tala wondered where she came from, all she had seen was the man and the monsters. "Maybe she was hiding in the trees" Tala thought as the man carefully laid the girl on the ground made and sure she was all right than walked toward Tala . "He sure is handsome" Tala thought as he walked toward her. He was the same age as her. His look reminded her of the movie Aladdin what did they call it "Arabian" his skin was a deep shade of bronze and He had deep blue eyes that stood out against his bright red hair. Now that she looked she reassessed her earlier impression his clothes where more like if an Arabian moved to Britain in the middle ages baggy but made for battle he told her his name and asked for hers "Tala, my name is Tala " she said

Aden laid the unconscious girl down to rest than went off to talk to the woman. The giant man was gone by the time he got there. There was a strange look to her as he approached her he decided she was an elf an exceedingly rare sight in Elysia these days. "Hello" he said "crazy circumstances but it is still nice to meet you we do not often get elves in these parts my name is Aden Elkgrove may I asked your name" after a pause she spoke "Tala, my name is Tala."

"May I ask what an elf is doing all by herself in these parts and on a full moon nonetheless" he said. "An elf I guess that's right my new look was very reminiscent of the elves I read about in my books" she thought. At this point Tala was pretty sure she had gone insane and was just going along with it. "Thanks for saving me I don't know why I'm here I went to bed at home and just woke up here, can you tell me where we are." "Well this is Slumbering Wood on the west coast of Elysia" you don't know it I thought all elves knew it as they did the back of their hands" said Aden. "No" said Tala. "Do you know where you're from then?" he asked. "Honestly I don't even think I'm on the same planet" said Tala. "Really that's a new one well I'll just have to help you get home then you're probably just lost this part of the wood is isolated and unfamiliar to outsiders, so you are from Elysia right" said Aden.

"I don't even know where that is" she responded. " Ooookay, well I've got a friend who might be able to help." "I don't know how to thank you enough for saving me and offering to help me get home" said Tala. "Think nothing of it" said Aden "its reward enough just to keep the company of an elf especially one as beautiful as you" Tala blushed. "I just have to see to the girl then go to my camp and get my things.

They both walked over to the girl "Who is she" asked Tala "One of the werewolves" said Aden. "Is that what attacked us?" Tala asked. "Yeah" said Aden "but don't worry they're harmless during the day time she won't change again until the next full moon." The girl awoke at the sound of Aden's voice "what happened did I kill anyone "said the girl. "No, but not for lack of trying" said Aden "how are you." "Hungry" said the girl "so where are the others" she said again she spoke in a harsh tone not befitting a girl that young it chilled Tala. "They went away and I don't think they'll be coming back" said Aden, attempting to be delicate. "So they're dead then" said the girl who did it rival pack, angry villagers, you two couldn't have managed it could you I supposed we deserved it killed your family or the like." "I'm sorry it was us we had…help" said Aden. "Look you don't need to talk to me like that I'm older then I look" said the girl. "How old?" said Tala. "14 if you must know elf girl" she said to Tala. She turned to Aden and asked matter of factually "Are you going to kill me?" "Uh, no, of course not" said Aden. "All right then can you point me in the direction of town." "It's that way" said Aden pointing south. The girl stood up dusted herself off and walked away without another word.

"Wait" said Tala stopping the girl half way through the clearing. As she was walking by the remnants of her former family. "What?" snapped the girl. "Why don't you come with us said" Tala. The girl seemed shocked then troubled by this.

"And you would have me knowing I am a monster and will try my best to eat you on the next full moon." "I couldn't live with myself if I let a little girl go off into the woods by herself." The girl considered it for a moment then drifted back to them somewhat aloofly. "You may yet regret your offer, but very well. I need a new pack, but I will not be treated as a child, remember my age." "All right" said Tala "but if we are going to travel together we must know your name." "It's Bella" said the girl. "Good I'm Tala and this is Aden." "Well now that were all acquainted can we go" said Bella in her grumpy voice. Aden did not seem put off nor did he seem upset that Tala had invited Bella along. "Sure" said Aden right this way Aden then lead three of them back to his camp.

"Sorry about your bird I saw what happened to it" Tala said to Aden on the way back to his camp. "What" said Aden "your bird he died in the fight didn't he." "Bird? Oh you mean Brand" said Aden. "He's not a bird, well he is but here I'll just show you all I need is some ashes. "When they got back to the camp Aden went over to the cooking fire he had used the previous night and dug up a handful of ash. he placed it on a nearby rock then leaned over it and muttered a few things she couldn't hear and quickly jerked his head up just as the pile burst into flame then morphed into the blazing red falcon Brand. He squawked happily feeling renewed and revitalized after his recent rebirth then he flew up onto Aden's shoulder. "*So you're alive*" he said in his flaming voice. "Wow that's a new one" Tala said amazed. "This is Brand" said Aden. "He's a phoenix that means he can be magically reborn from ashes." "*That doesn't mean it doesn't hurt so try not to get me killed next time.*" "Oh! It can talk, Hi my name is Tala" she said to the phoenix he did not respond. "Don't bother with him" said Aden "he doesn't talk to anyone besides me I don't even think he'd talk to me if he wasn't my familiar." "What's a familiar?" asked Tala. "You don't know"

Aden said surprised "you're a nature wizard aren't you, you just summoned a familiar a earlier, the Golem."

"So that's what that monster was they were less scary in my books" thought Tala. "I'm not a" she said "I mean I've never done magic, not before that thing, are you a wizard." "Yep ,and a first rate one too if I do say so myself I specialize in fire magic. anyway I thought for sure you were a great magician indeed to summon a golem. They are the strongest of the defensive nature familiars. There are very few magicians that can summon them even among the elves at least I assume. Well if you don't know magic I suppose I'll have to teach you on the way can't have an untrained wizard wandering around if you summoned a familiar that powerful on accident I don't want to see what kind of aggressor you could summon." "Aggressor?" " An aggressor familiar they're used for offense and can be quite nasty. I know I myself once accidentally summoned a nasty fire demon although I guess I am drifting from my point. It's hard to summon a benevolent familiar among the fire elementals. Most of them fire are evil even phoenix's they aren't evil but I wouldn't call them nice, so I wouldn't get my hopes up with brand he doesn't like anybody." *"that's not true I like the wolf girl she shares my aura"* said Brand *"what is your name girl."* "Bella, what is it to you pigeon." *"See that is what I mean" said Brand.* "Your bird talks too much" said Bella. Brand just made a noise that sounded like a giggle and took flight"

Aden watched brand go amazed "Brand that is the only person you have ever talked to besides me and master Kroft." Brand did not speak further he just alighted on Aden's shoulder looking deceptively like a normal bird despite the fact he was on fire. Turning to pack up his things Aden released the spell on his tent and it collapsed into a neat pile. Aden rolled up the tarp and strapped it to his pack. Then he said "alright ready to go, we have a half days walk to the Chaunt river than a two day boat ride to Callack city to see my friend Isaac. He should be able to help you Tala, and maybe even you Bella." "Who said I needed help arsonist." "Well she does have... let's call it spirit" Aden said to Brand "Okay then let's be off then" said Aden "normally I'd say we should get better acquainted over a drink but I think in this situation it is best if we make haste is that all right with you Tala?"

" Yeah sure" Tala was barely listening to him wizards and phoenixes, why not that seems about right considering the day so far. She was so amazed that she thought her shock would never end. At first she thought she was dreaming or crazy but now that she was more in tune with her new body she knew it was real and somehow she had been taken to a fantastic and terrifying new world. This was just like her adventure books. Suddenly she remembered the man she had thought up before falling asleep. Aden this wizard with me is the one that I thought of before I fell asleep. this troubled her could it be that it all really was a dream could it be that it all wasn't real or had she just gone crazy. It couldn't be that there's a coincidence that huge.

Tala spent the next half hour mulling over the fears she had and doubting her sanity when Aden interrupted her train of thought by saying "so Tala you said you did not know how you got to be in the forest nor why you were there or anything about this land then what do you remember?" "I remember going to sleep last night in my bed at home" said Tala. "Where is your home?" said Aden. "Nowhere near here not this place" "What land then what is it called?" said Aden. "I'm from new York city in the united states." "Hmm…I have not heard of either of those places it must be very far away and remote tell me more about it." said Aden. " I'd rather not say anything else Aden I don't want you to think I'm crazy." "If that is what you wish" said Aden "this is quite the mystery I will have it solved by the time we part this I promise you for curiosity is my greatest asset." "*You mean your greatest weakness I've never seen it do anything but get you into trouble*" said Brand. "Oh stop it you grumpy crow" said Aden. Tala giggled she was beginning to like the phoenix. "I find your presence here rather troubling also" said Bella. In her moody tone not specifying whether it was the circumstances that troubled her or simply Tala being there.

"Aden why don't you tell me about where we are." "well this" he said gesturing all around him in a large gesture is is the great kingdom of Elysia. We are currently in the Slumbering wood. To the south is Pakarr village. To the north is the Chaunt river which goes west from the ocean passing the Ælfwynn forest then the river leads to are destination the great Callack city in the middle of Elysia. To the northwest of Callack is the villages of the Vel which give way to the Dancar mountains. To the east of Callack is Shadow City and to the south is the Monde dessert." "and…" "are you going to go on forever she gets it" interrupted Bella . "Sorry I do tend to ramble" said Aden. "It didn't bother me said Tala and grabbed Aden's arm tell me more. At first Aden went stiff in her grasp then relaxed and continued walking while she held him. They talked the rest of the way to the river Bella even warmed up a little she dropped her constant insults and sarcasm but did not lose her abrasive voice and the snide manner she carried herself in ,which appeared so unnatural coming from such a small innocent looking girl, in the past if Tala had imagined a fragile innocent girl Bella would be what she would have pictured, not anymore.

As they walked Aden began to consider the position he had found himself in. Who was this girl he knew she was important that he had decided immediately. An elf revealing herself to a human it had not happened since long before he was born. Her appearing now had to mean something. Could she be connected to Raven, probably not but it was possible here appearance had almost coincided exactly with the rumors of Raven's resurfacing. Whether or not she was telling the truth which she almost assuredly wasn't the best thing he could do is to keep an eye on her and try to figure out her true motives.

The sun was just pasted its zenith when the group reached the Chaunt river the forest slowly dissolved into a small clearing next to the river. The river itself was huge the river was at least 1000 yards wide and probably half as deep judging from the deep blue color of the water. The water moved quickly and smoothly but it was dotted with many small whirlpools indicating hidden danger. She looked past the river and saw tall dense grassland on the other side extending all the way to the forest just visible on the edge of the horizon. She decided it must be the Ælfwynn forest that Aden had mentioned. Tala eyed the river she was a pretty good swimmer good enough that her gym teacher tried to recruit her onto the school team but her experience only made her want to swim across less. Aden saw her look of hesitation "pretty impressive isn't it and this is a spot were the river is thinnest" said Aden. "but don't worry we are not going to swim it that would be crazy and much slower Callack is very far downstream." "Then how are we traveling are you carrying a boat in your pants we don't know about" said Bella. "We'll sort of magical construction was one of my best subjects at the academy. I will have us a boat by nightfall said Aden. "Academy?" Tala looked at Aden ignorant of what he was speaking for the umpteenth time that day. "I did mention I was a wizard didn't I graduated top of my class I'll be able to build a boat with some spells but it will take a while it doesn't take much power but its complicated magic and take concentration. You should watch

Tala it should be a good learning experience for you it combines two kinds of magic fire and solid state morphing"

Aden walked over to a cluster of trees reached out with his hands toward the trees and spoke the words "vatra fasath". Ten thin red tendrils of fire streamed out of his hands and reached for the trees when they reached the bases of the trees they quickly burned through them. The trees then tipped and fell into a pile at his feet. The stumps and base on the timbers were singed black. The cuts the tendrils made were precise surgical like the cut was made by a giant flaming scalpel. Aden stood perfectly still as the tendrils continued on to shave the limbs of the trees and then cut each log down the middle making flat straight boards. The process released the scent burnt wood into the air. Then the tendrils formed a sort of hand and instead of cutting arranged the wood and disappeared. Then Aden raised both hands over the arrangement and muttered a stream of words so fast neither Tala or Bella could make them out. Nothing happened other than the wood slowly began to rattle. This part of the spell took the longest over the next hour he muttered faster and faster and the wood responded in kind rattling so hard that at its peak it was bouncing two feet of the ground. Finally when the sun was half way between the top of the sky and the horizon all the pieces of wood flew off the ground and came together the boards bending and twisting until it formed a long row boat and hung in the sky whole but still in separate pieces relaxed and lowered his hand the boat remained floating .

"That was morphing magic" said Aden "all wizards learn it regardless of their wizarding element I am almost done all I have to do is fuse the wood when I have finished we will eat supper then depart after night fall. Brand if you would be so kind as to get dinner" *"very well"* said brand and he flew off. Then Aden approached the boat which was still floating and began running his finger over the spaces in between the pieces of wood. Wherever he touched the boat the wood became fused a little over an hour later he had gone over the entire boat with his hands when he was done the boat was one giant seamless piece of wood. Then the boat suddenly back under the sway of gravity fell to the ground with a loud thud giving Tala and Bella a start. Aden sat down falling almost as hard as the boat clearly it had been quite the ordeal for him . "Wow that was amazing" said Tala "yeah I guess it was wasn't it" said Aden. "Yes I must I am also impressed" said Bella as she sat down next to Aden. "And just in time for dinner" Aden said "here comes brand"

Tala and Bella looked around but saw no signs of the phoenix over the next 5 minutes they continued to look around for the phoenix. During that time Aden just sat there sure of his statement despite the phoenix's continued absence. Tala was about to say something when she spotted brand in the distance carrying something in his talons. it wasn't until he came closer that she realized how much bigger he was then he had been before. He had grown to the size of an ostrich and now had a wing span at least 12 feet wide, he was carrying a full grown stag in his talons. "How was the hunting" said Aden as brand circled the group *"decent"* said brand. *"I caught a couple fire salamanders on the way"* brand dropped the stag in the middle of the group , quickly shrunk back to his normal size, flew to his perch on Aden's shoulder and began preening his flames.

"It looks good" said Aden "and the best part is we don't even have to cook it brand slow roasts it as he flies the meat will fall right off the bone. Aden pulled out a knife and skinned the deer "what cut do you want Tala." "I don't know" she said "I've never had deer." "Did you live in a cave your whole life" said Bella who hasn't had venison." "It is quite odd" said Aden "do elves not eat deer." "I don't know what elves eat" said Tala "and I've just never had deer I've… it's just you have to hunt deer and I lived in a city were there weren't any deer around" actually Tala didn't really care for animal mistreatment and was a vegetarian but with the things that had happened today she wasn't about to start objecting now. "Oh" said Aden "then I suggest this here its extra tender" he cut off a piece somewhere, Tala didn't know the name, and handed it to Tala. who ate it and smiled "It's really good, I didn't think it would be so tasty" she said. "Here have some more." Aden cut off a larger piece of the buck and handed it to Tala then he turned to Bella and said "what would you like Bella" "I'll have the heart and the kidneys" Bella said . When they looked at her surprised she shied away from their gaze. "When you've been a werewolf as long as I have you gain some odd tastes, it's not all bad though my senses are much sharper than a normal human's" she kept her gaze off them clearly upset Tala walked over to Bella and put her hand around her. "Why don't you tell us about it, how did you get like this."

They finished eating and listened while Bella talked to them "I've been a werewolf as long as I can remember maybe my whole life I never knew my parents, but that's not the only thing . I'm not the same as other people even the werewolves in my pack for one thing I age half as fast as normal people, werewolves included. Even the other werewolves I lived with, my pack were distant from me and there are other things..." Bella trailed off when she did not continue Tala spoke. "That sounds horrible" said Tala "is that kind of thing common here." It was Aden that answered her "werewolves are common enough, lycanthropy , or the werewolf's curse has plagued Elysia for all of recorded history, but the slow aging I've never heard of anything like it outside of elves it must have been caused by being changed at such a young age I can't be sure however I am not an expert." "You can help her though right"

Tala asked. " I am not going to lie the odds are slim I have never heard of a werewolf being cured but if there is any help at all we can find for her we will find it in Callack." Bella laughed "there is no cure, but that is fine I am resigned to my fate I would be more upset if there was a cure and nobody ever told me." "You can't talk like that Bella there's always hope" said Tala. "Do not act like you know my pain, you will see, you offer me your companionship and I will take it but when the next full moon comes around either you will kill me or I will kill you that is just how it is."

There was silence for a longtime after Bella's proclamation until Aden interrupted in an urgent tone. "Well we better get going its well after nightfall they loaded the boat with their meager possessions, then Tala and the others pushed the boat to the edge of the river "alright" said Aden " everybody in." Without hesitation they climbed in the boat and took off it was surprisingly roomy on board. "Okay it's two days by boat to Callack said Aden I've preserved some venison for us to eat on the way and Tala I suggest you get some sleep because we start your training tomorrow at dawn."The boat was wide enough for the three of them to sleep abreast Tala slept in the middle while Aden and Bella slept on the sides.

Tala and Bella had no trouble sleeping, the day had held lots of stress and disheartening realizations for them neither of them where travelers and although Bella was used to this land and its hardships the journey had been far harder on her small body than Tala's tall strong elf one especially after her transformation. Aden on the other hand was more than used to this type of thing he was constantly moving, so at the end of the day he was no worse for wear so sleep did not come as easy to him, but in truth it never did. Aden was plagued by nightmares, torturous dreams of his past, he was awoken in the middle of the night after a particularly nasty one. He lurched upright in the boat when he felt Tala next to him he smiled amused that he had forgotten about his new companions as frightened as he was by his dream. *"A little jumpy aren't we"* Brand raised his head from the seat at the stern of the boat were he had chosen to roost. Aden did not answer him he just laid back down glad that he had not woken Tala and Bella . Brand said nothing else and instead put his head back down and went to sleep although he'd never admit it Aden knew Brand worried about him.

Aden laid on the boat awake for a while and thought about the strange events that had befallen him up to this point. Aden did not take on companions lightly he had had his own motives for befriending Tala elves were supposed to know more about the nature of magic than any other creature, but they had been isolated closed off from the rest of the world for almost a century. Tala could be the in he needed, Aden had hoped she could tell him the reason for the dark magic that had been creeping into the world and if it was related to his past. Of course it was his bad luck that he found the only elf that didn't even know who she was, let alone do magic. If she was even telling the truth and even if she was he reasoned she had to know more than she remembered and maybe he could bring those memories back with the right help. Bella was definitively not a friend he would have made but he did not object when Tala told her to come with them because it was clearly important to her and he had expected Bella to refuse. After that it was too late to do anything. He was weary of having a werewolf with him but when Brand took such a liking to her he decided she must be a very special person ,though that is not necessarily mean she is a good one. Aden thought as he fell back asleep and drifted into the world of nightmares that had replaced the hopeful dreams for the future that he had had as a child.

Tala awoke the next morning to a light that was so bright

that even through her eyelids it was as though she was staring at the sun. She opened her eyes just a crack and saw it was Brand standing on the seat at the stern of the boat. He had his wings fully spread and was emitting a blinding light after a few moments the light receded like a supernova collapsing in on itself revealing the phoenix standing there looking around happily. Tala groaned and rubbed her eyes "what was that" she turned to Aden who was sitting up yawning he smiled. "Well you know how roosters crow at dawn Phoenixes are a little more flashy."

Tala looked around as the spots faded from her eyes the slumbering wood was still on the right bank but the left bank was all hills mixed with the grasslands she saw where they first entered the river however the Ælfwynn forest was nowhere to be seen it had given way to grassy plains. They had a quick breakfast of venison and some nuts and berries Bella had gathered before they left. "Not even a werewolf can survive on meat alone I like variety" she had said. "I can't believe how well I slept last night I'm so used to beds and pillows" said Tala. "It is true I am used to meager bedding even bare ground but rarely have I slept so soundly" Bella agreed. "It's the magic the boat is soaked in residual energy direct contact has comforting effects unfortunately I've built up and immunity and what was left has mostly dissipated sleep tonight will not be as pleasant." for the remainder or the meal Bella stared intensely at Aden finally he grew fed up "why are you staring at me." Bella unfazed by his outburst replied coolly "you are hiding something." Aden huffed "I am hiding somthing, I don't know what you're talking about." "my animal half makes me exceptionally intuitive and you are remaining emotionally distant the way you talk it's too elegant and unemotional you never reveal how you are feeling, it means your hiding something." "Listen Bella" "don't worry" Bella interrupted "everyone deserves the right to keep their secrets. I just didn't want you thinking you had got something by me. You can keep your secret mystery man" Aden didn't reply instead deciding to let the issue drop. Tala was confused by the whole exchange and remained silent. "She is definitely special" Aden thought "she is quite intelligent I better keep an eye on her as well"

After they finished breakfast Aden cleared a small space on the boat "shall we start our training then" said Aden to Tala. "It is very important that you are trained they say there is nothing more dangerous than an untrained wizard and with your power it is essential we get your magic under your control before you accidentally kill us all.

Aden and Tala sat cross legged across from each other in the middle of the boat Bella sat in Brand's seat at the back of the boat and Brand begrudgingly perched on the arm rest fighting the urge to peck the intruder on his previous perch. "The first step to becoming a magician is finding your magic." said Aden. "Though concentration and meditation you have to center in and isolate the magical source inside that all wizards possess then you have to create a mental pathway to it so you can tap into it easily when you need it." "What is the magic like" said Tala "how do I find it, and how will I know when I've found it." "Oh trust me you'll know" said Aden. "I know that it is an odd concept but if you concentrate and feel deep inside your being you will succeed I promise and I'll be right here monitoring your progress." "Okay I'll try" Tala closed her eyes and concentrated.

Tala never felt more self concious in her life. What was she doing this is ridiculous, but what did she know magic was real she'd seen it hadn't she and the golem that had been her. At least that's what Aden said. Maybe if she thought about what happened maybe she had felt something. She might as well try so she looked deep inside herself searching for the magic at first she thought she might find it then the more she concentrated and searched the more elusive here quarry became. She just didn't feel anything magical. eventually her mind began to wander and she just started visiting old memories of good times in her life , Christmas and birthdays and even a few she did not know she had like her mother reading to her when she was young. Suddenly Tala grew sad and her concentration completely broke as she wondered if she would ever see her father again. Tala tried for a few more moments than opened her eyes.

"It's no good" she said "I can't find anything magical." "Aden did not open his eyes apparently he had joined her in meditation. "Try again" he said "I know you can do it nobody said it would be easy it does take time." "Okay" she said Tala closed her eyes and again attempted looking inside herself. She sat there quietly for the next twenty minutes then opened her eyes again. "I just can't! "She said. This time Aden opened his eyes. "She's is only looking superficially she doesn't really believe" he thought "I have to make her go deeper." "I was afraid I'd have to do this" he said shifting to speaking outside his head. "What?" said Tala. "Look into my eyes" he said. "She did, she was thinking about what a beautiful shade of blue they were when he snapped his fingers and she fell forward onto her face unconscious. "What did you do to her?" asked Bella. "I put her in a deep meditative state.Though I probably should have caught her. That's going to hurt when she wakes up" said Aden. "This way she will be forced to find her magic in order to get out." "What If she doesn't" said Bella. "She probably won't at least not on the first try, but don't worry I can take her out of it" said Aden "all it takes is a snap but that's not the problem." "Then what is?" "Even though she doesn't know it she is a strong wizard I'm sure she will find her magic but her being in this state is dangerous." "What could happen to her?"

"It's not dangerous for her it's dangerous for us." Finished talking Aden closed his eyes again and resumed his position in order to monitor Tala's progress. they sat like that for several hours and Bella was about to ask for lunch when they heard a shriek Bella and Aden turned to see several winged creatures coming towards them.

Tala was surrounded by darkness but it was familiar darkness the darkness of her mind. What did he do to me she thought. "Find your magic" she heard Aden's voice in her mind. "Aden "she yelled he didn't respond. "Okay guess I don't have a choice" she thought and she dug deep ignoring small memories and thoughts in search of something deeper. For hours she prowled the recesses of her mind and found nothing. Then suddenly warmth began to wash over her and she knew she was close. She could feel that she was just about to reach it when she was yanked violently out of her dream world and slowly came into consciousness on the other side and she found herself in the middle of a raging battle.

Their boat was being descended on by what appeared to be giant owls. Aden was swinging wildly at their legs with his sword which was currently on fire fending them off, but they were clearly not frightened, nor did Aden succeed in harming them other than some minor cuts and bruises. "What the hell is going on here!" shouted Tala. Aden squeezed out one word in between quick breaths "Strix."

One of the Strix split from the pack and swooped towards Bella. Reacting fast almost purely on instinct like she had with the wolves the previous night Tala drew her sword and managed to cut one of the beast's legs off. It shrieked in pain and flew away Tala joined Aden and began swinging at the rest of the attackers. Even though she had almost no experience for some reason she did much more damage than Aden. She cut off a talon here, clipped a wing there, but there were still too many of them. Their situation seemed hopeless Aden had been slashed several times and he was clearly tiring. Tala was starting to get tired too with every swing it was like she was swinging a 100 pound weight. Suddenly the fire on Aden's sword went out he no longer had the energy to maintain the blaze. This seemed to embolden the Strix they seemed to attack even harder. One gave Tala a gash across her arm she stumbled backward and twisted her ankle. Another attacked her and she fell. The remaining Strix turned to Aden. He was overwhelmed he became covered in hundreds of cuts and scrapes in a matter of seconds, his resistance to the creature's assault grew even weaker. They were coming at him like piranha in a feeding frenzy. Brand tried to help him but was batted away and just as the wizard was fading out of consciousness he saw a bright light and new his time had come.

Tala panicked she didn't know what to do Bella came over to help her up but it was too late the harpies were tearing Aden apart. Whenever they tried to approach and help Aden they were battered easily aside. Just as all hope seemed lost the unthinkable happened a huge ball off energy flew in from the shore and struck the monsters, it blasted them out of the sky they landed on the shore 50 yards away burnt to a crisp. Tala, Aden, and Bella just stared shocked "what just happened?" asked Tala. Before anyone could answer their boat turned seemingly of its own accord floated over to the shore and beached itself they tried to steer it but to no avail .when they landed Tala looked around. There was not a thing in sight besides grass. She realized with a shock that Aden was unconscious lying on his back at the front end of the boat. Bella was already kneeling next to him trying to wake him up. Brand was standing on his chest just staring at Aden's closed eyes. Tala stood there for a moment and examined his injuries he had a big gash above his brow that went all the way to his temple and the eye below was already beginning to turn black and blue. he had several deep looking cuts on his torso and she suspected he had matching ones on his back but his arms were the worst his shirt was completely ripped to the shoulders and his bracers had even been torn off he had cuts that covered his arm with increasing severity as you got to his hands. His hands where a barely recognizable shredded bloody mess. Tala walked over to Aden and knelt beside him having trouble trying to find the word she wanted to say. She finally settled with "Aden are you okay!" At the sound of her voice Aden woke up "you're okay" Bella exclaimed happily.

  "Well of course I'm okay" said Aden "you think a couple of birds could do me in" said Aden. "*Yes*" said Brand sarcastically. "Oh shut up" "are you okay" repeated Tala "a few minor scratches" said Aden. He grimaced when he looked at what was left of his hands. "Good thing I shielded myself though, better my hands wounded than my face thanks for the help Tala. I have to ask how did you harm them they were heavily warded against weapons and magic. They had to have been sent by some dark wizard, strix make good assassin's they can sense magic being used." "I don't know how I did it, I just did." "Hmm yet another mystery." "It's no mystery elven swords are specially crafted to counter all forms of magic and enchantments" interrupted an unknown voice. They all spun to see a small elderly man standing a little of to the distance. Startled they all stood up and faced the stranger then they found they were no longer in the boat in fact it had seemed to have disappeared entirely leaving them standing on the shore. Aden spoke first "who are you what do you want" he said. "Who me" the man pointed to himself "I am your fate." he smiled and stroked his beard. "Did you save us" said Bella. "Ah very astute young werewolf yes I am the one who saved you." "then why did you take our boat?" Aden demanded. "because reaching Callack by boat is not your destiny." "How do you know so much how do you know about Bella about our trip?" "I know many thing s, before we talk any further" the old man approached Aden "let me heal those wounds, since Tala has not yet discovered her abilities." "I don't..." before Aden could argue the man waved his hand and a glorious blue light illuminated Aden. Slowly his flesh began to nit itself back together leaving no trace of the cuts behind. The magic even washed away his blood and repaired his clothing. Then the light faded Aden stared in amazement at himself. Not only was he healed he felt better than he ever had in his entire life.

"That was the most powerful healing magic I've ever seen" said Aden "to use a spell like that without saying words and to not even appear tired afterward you must be one of the most powerful wizards in the world." "Perhaps" said the man "but in the end such things are unimportant." "Thanks a lot but I have to ask why did you save us who are you" Aden asked. "Who I am is unimportant, what I do is ensure you meet your fate, and I couldn't let those filthy creatures interfere could I." "what does that mean." without warning the man threw up an arm and shot a small ball of blue energy at Bella that hit her square in the chest. she went rigged and fell to the ground with a thud" Aden threw his hands up to make a shield but was to slow and a ball caught him in the shoulder and he collapsed his left arm paralyzed." then the old turned to Tala he hesitated for a moment before throwing his hands up again. Giving Tala enough time to pull her sword out just as the wizard shot more energy from his hands. Tala could do nothing but watch and pray as the ball soared at her and struck the sword then appeared to disappear inside of it.

The stranger chuckled "very good you remembered what I said you will survive I'm sure of it but listen to me, unless you find the others that have come here like you. You will not survive long not with the dark one loose in the world." "What others what are you talking about" asked Tala. "You don't think you are the only one who came to this world. you are special though you have to find the others and..." the old wizard was interrupted as an enormous ball of intense flames tore through the field and struck the wizard head on with the force of a bullet train then plowed on leaving nothing behind it but ash until it vanished in the distance. There was no trace of the old mysterious wizard left behind.

Tala let out a sigh of relief too tired to be surprised by the sudden change of circumstances. "Are you okay said Aden. "Yeah" said Tala "how about you did you get hit by that light." "Yeah I'm kind of curious about that I'm familiar with that spell, I have seen it once. it's one of the most powerful spells there is a blast of pure energy I should be dead 5 times over but I'm fine I just had temporary paralysis from the magic overload." "I'm okay too" said Bella running over to them. Tala let out a huff "do they treat all newcomers to Elysia this way I haven't gone 5 minutes without being attacked since I got here?" "Just the special guests Tala, but don't worry it will calm down I promise" said Aden "who was that guy asked Bella. " I don't know but I think that man knew about me about why I'm here" said Tala "He said there were others and something about a dark one. He was saying more but then you, ya know." "Oh, sorry" said Aden "I had to finish him while I could." "You *know he's not dead*" said brand. "He's not where is he" said Tala surprised she looked around. "I don't see him are you sure?" *"Yes he escaped I swear human eyes are useless I don't know how you live with them"* said brand. "It doesn't surprise me" said Aden "That wizard was crazy powerful using just one of those energy spells takes enough energy to kill a normal man he used 3 and seemed none the worse for it." "I do not like it" said Bella "he knew too much he might be following us." "So what do we do now asked Tala" eager to be away from the place they had fought the strange wizard "our boat is gone" said Bella "I know" said Aden "the wizard must have sent it away." "You can make another one though can't you" asked Tala. "No" said Aden "I used too much energy making the fireball. I won't be able to use that kind of magic for several days and besides I think it is dangerous for us to continue to travel by the river someone summoned the Strix to attack us and dangerous as he may be I don't think it was the wizard we just encountered.Whoever it was they are still out there they might do it again." "So" said Bella "we must travel by land" "yes I think that is best" he answered "how long a walk is it to Callack" asked Tala. "I'm not sure a several day journey" he said. "Then we better get going we're wasting sunlight" said Bella.

          To Tala's relief they quickly moved on. She felt like she was being watched where they were and it was giving her the creeps. They got though the rest of the day without incident. The terrain was a lot easier to travel here than it was in the forest, although the hot sun pressed in on them as they walked, and they frequently stopped at the river to drink. It was a little after dark when Aden finally let them stop to camp. Again he sent out Brand to get something to eat this time he came back with a fox and a rabbit. It was slim pickings out in the plains not like in the forest. The fox was a little tough but the rabbit was good. Tala was somewhat averse to her new exotic diet at first but everything seemed to be going well. Bella had gone in search of berries and fruits again this time Tala helped, but she seemed to do more harm than good, because most of the things she picked were poisonous. After diner they talked a little then went to sleep.

          That night Tala dreamed about the magic she had almost grasped from deep inside. She dreamed she had found it and it was amazing. She felt the power it was hotter than the strongest fire, but icy at the same time cool and refreshing. With a sense of great strength but more than anything there was this enormous light that shone pure green. That she somehow felt instead of saw. Then all of a sudden it was gone and she drifted back into the endless darkness of the realm of sleep.

She woke up the next morning to Aden's face yelling at her. "Tala! He yelled stop it, stop it, get these things off of me." she stared at him drowsily and quickly sobered up, to her surprise Aden was completely covered in thorny vines that continued to envelope and constrict his body. "Undo the spell" he yelled. "What spell! What spell how! " Tala said. "Look around you Tala." She looked around and saw that not just Aden, but the entire clearing was covered in the thick vines. Including Bella who was giving her nasty looks but could not voice her outrage due to a particularly large vine that was gagging her. The vines continued to spread Tala however was completely untouched. She lay protected in the middle as the vines radiated outward from her then it dawned on her. "I did this" she said. "Yes! Aden said now please try to undo it this hurts replied a frustrated Aden. Tala had no idea how to go about undoing the spell. So she drew her sword and began the slow process of cutting the vines off her companions. As soon as she stood up the vines stopped spreading but did not disappear. when she got Aden loose he joined in ,but even with his help the morning was half over by the time Bella, brand and there supplies were cut out of the enormous pile of vines they might not have even found brand if he hadn't been on fire.

Aden straightened holding his back he was still panting from all the hacking and chopping. "That" he said between gasps" is why you have to train magicians we need to find your magic before we all get killed." "I found it already, well in a dream" said Tala. "While I was sleeping I saw it at least I think

I did." A quick look went across Aden's that looked like pain. "Are you sure about that" he asked giving her a serious look. "Can you find it again?" "I think so" said Tala. "She calmed herself and looked inside her being the way she had in her dream and sure enough she found her magic. The huge presence resting in the place she had discovered it while she was sleeping. It was hard to believe she had had such a difficult time finding it. The power now seemed to dominate her. "Yes I found it" she said. "Okay now listen carefully Tala I want you to concentrate on the magic and say "Aparo" okay. "Okay" she said. "I'll try it Tala drew in a deep breath, closed her eyes, and concentrated on the magic. Then spoke the word Aparo. Tala opened her eyes just as she burst into a magnificent green flame as bright as brand at dawn. The green inferno felt surprisingly calm and cool and gave off the scent of pine needles. The ghost fire began to slowly recede, but Tala still retained a slight green glow for a while after that. "Congratulations" Aden said you've passed the first level of training your power should be under control from now on." He paused then he said "I have only ever heard of one other person in the history magic who discovered their magic while in their sleep. He was a... "Classmate" of mine when I was an apprentice his name is Raven. You don't know him by any chance." The name sounded extremely familiar to Tala but she could not place it and at last she said "no, I don't know him." "Then is it an elf thing" asked Aden. "Sorry I don't know anything about magic." "Ah I see" Aden looked at Tala suspiciously then turned and walked away mulling over the events of the morning.

He started to make breakfast. Brand landed on his shoulder. Bella walked over to Tala and pointed her finger an inch from Tala's eye "I don't care if you were awake or not. Use magic on me again, and it will be the last time" she said then left to go sit next to Aden, while he was making breakfast. They said little while eating then they packed up and kept hiking. Tala spent the rest of the day feeling like an outsider .Aden seemed to be lost in self-reflection, and Bella had not spoken to her since the scary confrontation that morning so Tala was thoroughly depressed by the time they made camp that night. That night they had rabbit for diner. Aden said nothing though the entire diner. He just sat there staring off into the distance. Then to Tala's surprise Bella got up from her usual spot as close to Aden as she could get and sat next to Tala. "you know I like you" she said "I know we've only known each other a short time, but I already like you much better than I did my old pack. I know I've acted horribly. I guess living with werewolves makes you cynical. Also I have this thing about being confined to small places." Tala gave her a grin "are you saying sorry." Bella smiled back "never, so anyway what's the deal with you and Aden" said Bella.

Aden was shocked out of his contemplative coma by the sound of frantic whispering and giggling coming from the right of him. He looked over and saw something he would have never guessed he would see in a thousand years. To his right an elf and a werewolf were in the woods huddled up whispering like a couple of school girls. They stopped talking for a moment then looked at Aden they grew beat red and resumed their conversation. "Women" Aden thought "no matter what the species they confound me."

Aden walked over to them. "Well it's nice to see you two getting along. Bella looked at him and blushed. "So Tala" he said "I appreciate your help with the Strix but it's apparent that you need to be trained in more than just magic. How about a little sword play before bed for practice." "Okay" said Tala hesitantly. "Good, I just need to ward us before we begin. It will keep us from getting wounded" Aden placed a protective spell on Tala, but since Tala's elven blade could cut though any

spell he did not bother to put any spells on himself. He would
have to hope his experience was enough because he could not
tell Tala he wasn't warded for fear she would hold back. Aden
gave her a few basic instructions. Then they both drew their
swords and squared off. "remember to plant your feet how I
showed you" Aden said "and try not to leave yourself open,
okay now strike at me " .Tala lunged at Aden her blade aimed
straight at his heart. Aden questioned the wisdom of leaving
himself unprotected, the attack was much more precise then he
expected from her but she had made a mistake. Her attack had
left her wide open and he spun to the side let her pass and
stabbed her in the back. Right between her ribs on her left were
her heart should be. The sword tip stopped an inch from her
back but sunk in like he had hit an invisible wall of rubber.
"Ow!" Tala said "I thought it wasn't supposed to hurt." "What I
said was you wouldn't be wounded I didn't say it wouldn't
hurt" Aden smiled. She swung angrily at his head he ducked
under it ready for the strike and swooped in to "kill" her a
second time, but to Aden's surprise she countered his counter
and swung again. They continued to spar long after dark. Much
longer then Aden had planned. He had "killed" her 4 more
times but eventually Aden had to call it of when Tala started
coming within an inch of really killing him with every strike.

The following morning Aden had a taste for hunting so
instead of sending brand out he went himself, although brand
flew overhead with his flame low scanning the land from above
for him to give him the edge over his prey. *"Why are you doing
all this for them"* brand said. "I told you" Aden said "I think
Tala will have some valuable information and I see you have no
objection to the werewolf." *"She is fine but not worth all the
effort you don't have to do so much for them. "* "Well the truth is
I've grown somewhat fond of them whether Tala is lying or not
and I've about had it with your sour attitude." *"I …I just don't*

want to see you risking your life for strangers is all." "Brand are you worried about me." *"Perhaps, I am your familiar after all I should be."* "well you don't have to worry you know I can take care of myself and....bizer !" a tiny bolt of lightning flew out of his finger and struck a deer that had stuck its head out some three hundred yards away directly in the temple killing it instantly. "Aha!" Aden jumped "who needs a bow see brand I can take anything on and win, line 'em up and I'll knock 'em down." Brand had missed Aden's cocky attitude that he seemed to have lost over the last week. It was the main reason he worried he found Aden's sudden change in mood reassuring.

They finished breakfast back at the camp and set off again all in good spirits. Tala had discovered the previous night that her new senses made Aden's movements appear slow. It was as if she was fighting a snail. If it wasn't for Aden's amazing skill with a sword she was sure she would have beaten him. It was frustrating fighting a man who barely seemed to move, but always managed to evade your attack. If that wasn't enough some of the places he had stabbed her still hurt even with his spell. "I'll beat him next" time she vowed to herself.

After a long day of hiking they made camp. The hilly terrain had given way to flat plains with patches of trees sprinkled about. "We are almost to Callack" said Aden. "It should be only a day's walk away see." Aden pointed off in the distance. There was a blurry gray line across the entire horizon and what appeared to be a mountain behind it. "What is it" asked Tala. "The city wall and the central city." "The whole thing!" she asked. "Yes the city is a grand sight to behold you'll see."

They made camp there, after diner Aden and Tala spared again. While they were sparing Bella got the urge to go for a walk and trotted off into the night. "Ahh!" Aden let out a yelp Tala had managed to stab Aden in the upper arm. "Oh! I'm sorry I'm sorry" she said in a panicked fluster. "I thought you were protected." The cut was deep at least 2 inches and was bleeding profusely. "Don't be" he said starting to look pale. "I shouldn't have underestimated you so much not to protect myself. Brand! Little help I'm in need of assistance." Brand flew over and landed on Aden's shoulder and rubbed his head across the wound. Aden yelled in pain. "What are you doing!" screamed Tala, but when brand raised his head she saw that his wound had been cauterized steam was rising from the scar it left behind. "I should be okay" Aden said "I'm just glad you only got my arm." Tala ran over and embraced Aden in a tight hug he grimaced in pain. "I'm so glad you're okay I was aiming for your neck" tears were streaming down her face. "It's okay it's okay" he held her. "I told you it was my fault and I have to tell you you're squeezing me little tight it hurts." Tala quickly let go "sorry" she blushed. Aden let out a big breath "now I think I need to go to bed" he said though heavy breathing. Then he dropped in his tent he was clearly in pain. Tala was worried about him so she stayed up as late as she could then just before she fell asleep she thought she saw several men completely black from head to toe she blinked and they vanished all she saw were shadows .

Bella meandered around for a little bit enjoying the view of the landscape at night. She was on her way back when she heard a rustling in the bushes she turned just in time to catch a black shape flash by. "Who's there "Bella yelled while spinning trying to locate the shadow in the night. All of a sudden Bella heard a crack from the ground beneath her, and then she dropped. Bella plummeted at least 20 feet, but landed safely in a small pile of brush on a small square stone platform. It cushioned her fall however she was still quite jolted by the descent. Groaning she reached around looking for something to pull herself up with. Suddenly she heads a sort of clicking noise. She stopped moving and listened tck. tck. tck .tck .tck. tck .tck. Tck......the ticking stopped for a moment. Then was followed by the loud echoing boom of a stone mechanism locking into place. Before Bella had a chance to move the platform suddenly flipped vertically and dumped her down a chute. It was long and took her deep into the earth. After a while the angle of the chute leveled out and ended.

It dumped her in a corridor. It was lighter here then it had been on the platform. She had become considerably sore and she rubbed herself as she stood up. To her surprise there was a lit torch on the wall next to her. She wondered how it had stayed lit when there was clearly no one to maintain it. She decided it was beyond her and it didn't really matter. She took it and held it so she could see the corridor in front of her. She was suddenly glad for her small stature. Aging at half the rate of normal humans had caused her more than a few problems in the past. However this corridor seemed to be made especially for someone her height. A normal sized person like Tala or Aden would have to crouch in order to avoid hitting their heads on the ceiling. Thinking back to the chute she fell down it was also small so small that a grown person could easily become stuck. Bella shook her head and put out of her mind chalking it up to happenstance. She started walking, there was no way she was getting back the way she came.

As she walked she noticed the hallway had carvings all along the wall. She stopped and put the torch up to one. It was a depiction of a werewolf. It had it arms held high and in its hands there appeared to be a baby. Moving on she saw the baby in several more carvings. In each one it was in a crowd growing older from carving to carving but never catching up with the crowd. She moved on and saw several more carvings. One was of a man turning into a werewolf under a full moon then of him turning back the next day surrounded by the dead with a look of sadness on his face. Bella did not think it was possible to capture that feeling, her feelings, in stone. She stared into the man's face until she tasted tears on her lips. His was a pain that all werewolves understood. Bella herself had no idea how many people she'd killed over the years. The only mercy you get as a werewolf is that you don't remember what happens that one night every month. She moved on but the rest of the carvings didn't seem to make sense. The next one showed the same man under a full moon but he was human and smiling. The final picture was a werewolf and a human standing together and the sun was out which was just impossible.

She absorbed this and moved on. About ten feet further down the corridor   it opened up into a large chamber. In the middle of the chamber stood a large statue of the werewolf god Luna. The perfect combination of wolf and man somehow more wolf like and more human at the same time than ordinary werewolves. Even with her wolven features she surpassed the beauty of any mortal woman. All other werewolves were ugly monsters compared to her. People had long since stopped worshiping her. Werewolves hated the idea she even existed and had willfully passed the curse onto humanity. The god's left hand was resting on a statue of a dragon. Even though dragons are the fiercest beasts in the mortal realm it seemed no more than a puppy compared to the god. Then something caught her eye.

Something in the dragon's mouth was reflecting the torchlight. She went over to it and reached inside. She pulled out the object and looked at it. It was a necklace. The chain was a strong but common metal tin or iron the pendant however was a large clear crystal in the shape of a crescent moon. With a perfect ruby set in the inner contour of the moon. The necklace seemed to call to her. She put it on without thinking. Bella's thoughts were interrupted by a crash as the statue of the goddess suddenly toppled over and smashed on the ground. revealing a hidden passage Bella examined the passageway it was bare and went up at a steep incline. Even from there she could see the pale moonlight leaking from outside this was definitely an exit.

She wasted no time and sprinted up the tunnel eager to escape the odd catacombs and get back to Tala and Aden The passage opened up into a crevice in a small rocky outcropping. It was really quite ingenious of whoever had created the temple. The entrance would be absolutely invisible to anyone who was not literally on top of it. Bella squeezed though the rock and made her way onto the outcropping. It was a tiny plateau in the wilderness. She could see for miles in every direction the grasslands had little to block her view, but she still could not locate the camp. She was pondering her next move when she heard a noise behind her, and everything went black.

When Tala woke up she instantly knew something was wrong. Aden was already up surveying the camp he was looking around troubled. When Tala got up she realized that the camp had been disturbed. Bella's bedding was unused and she was nowhere to be seen. "Where's Bella" Tala asked Aden. "I don't know, she may have left. She didn't seem exactly found of us, but it is strange brand is gone too." He thought for a moment "let's see if brand knows anything" Aden walked over to the campfire and scooped up some ash he repeated the incantation that had brought brand back before. Again brand burst into fiery life standing on Aden's hand. "Ah, so you were dead" said Aden. *"I'm alright thanks for asking"* he said. "Okay what happened then." *"I don't know. I felt a presence but could not see anything and before I could alert you I was struck dead. I never saw anyone."* "Now I'm even more troubled could it have been an act could Bella have felt so little for us that she killed brand just to leave undetected. It seems unlikely, but if we were attacked why did they leave Tala and I" said Aden "I need to think on this" he turned away from Tala then looked back. "In any case don't worry Tala Bella's strong she can take care of herself until we find her." However Tala was worried and she was also hurt. Could Bella have left them? If anything she thought that Bella was growing closer to them why would she suddenly up and leave. No it had to be something else.

Bella awoke in complete darkness she looked around but it was pointless there was not a speck of light. She attempted to sit up and discovered she could not move. She was being held completely immobile. So she endeavored to discover what information she could gather with her senses. Those senses combined with the amount of heavy breathing she was doing told her she was in a very small place. Probably some sort of box. "Hello can anybody hear me Aden, Tala, are you there!" Bella received no answer she spent the next several minutes calling for help and shouting threats to would be kidnappers, but she still received no response. Finally she gave up and relaxed. That's when she realized that she was moving but it felt unnatural. It was too smooth there were no bumps. She couldn't be on any cart or boat. It was as if she was merely moving through the air. Like when the old wizard had carried their boat off the river, and then something happened that made Bella feel something she had not felt in years. Fear.

"But we have to go there's nothing here. No trail to go on. I can't track her." Aden was trying to persuade Tala it wasn't going well. "But we can't just leave and go to Callack not while Bella is gone. What if she didn't just leave she could have been kidnapped or be in danger..." "I have neither magic nor any mortal means to find her. We have already searched for her. There is nothing more we can do here. However there may be something we can do once we get to Callack. We have to go and just hope she stays safe until we can find her, but there's a good chance she just left on her own. Werewolves aren't used to this kind of relationship you heard the way she talked." "Maybe at first, but what about the things she shared, especially last night she would not have shared those things with me if she wasn't fond of us." "That may be, but regardless my point stands. It is best to go to Callack. Tala was uncertain she did not want to leave but she thought Aden knew more when it came to these things. They would just have to go and hope that Bella stayed safe. "Okay" she said "then there is no time to waste" Tala stomped out of the camp at a pace Aden had trouble keeping up with.

The Great City of Callack

Due to Tala's quick eager pace they reached Callack well before sundown that day.
However when she got there Tala stood outside the city gates stunned. She did not notice Aden run up behind her panting. When she saw the city from camp the previous night she was sure it must have been a trick of the eyes and the city could not be as big as it looked but it was bigger. The city walls stretched as far as she could see in either direction and rose over ten stories high reaching for the sky. "Quite a sight isn't it said Aden. "I remember the first time I saw it, Callack the city in the mountain." "The city in the mountain?" Said Tala. "Yes before Callack was a city it was a mountain and if you thought the wall is amazing just wait till you see the mountain. Anyway the man we are here to see lives there in the middle of the city. Come on we have to get going it's a long way to the mountain. Oh, and make sure to keep your hood up if people see an elf

there will be…complications.""" okay" she said and covered her head and arms. Tala and Aden approached the enormous gates. There were many people coming in and out the first she'd seen other than Aden and Bella since arriving in Elysia.

When they reached the entrance a guard stopped them. "What business do you two have in Callack?" Aden flipped down his hood "we seek an audience with the wizard scholar Issac" said Aden. "Aden Elkgrove I am so sorry I didn't recognize…" "it's okay you are just doing your job, may we enter." "Of course, yes, please come in and enjoy your stay in Callack city" The guard stammered and waved them in. Tala watched this with interest. Apparently ass kissing was as popular in this world as in hers and Aden was way more important here than she thought. "What was that" Tala asked as Aden hailed a carriage to get them to the mountain. The driver was as nervous and flattering as the guard was. "What was what", "are you famous", "oh well kinda my um teacher was. It kind of carried over to us." "Us" "me and ….oh never mind, we better get going." Aden hopped into the carriage avoiding her gaze. She climbed up and sat next to Aden. The carriage was surprisingly comfortable all things considered. After she was seated Aden instructed the driver to depart and he snapped the reigns urging the horses onward. The carriage was faster than walking but it still took them over 5 hours to reach the base of the mountain.

The city was vast and more advanced architecturally then Tala had expected. Many buildings were 2 and 3 stories high. There were even a few up to six or seven stories as they got closer to the center of the city. They were all made of the same creamy white stone and decorated simply with matching red awnings. It had the uniform and homemade look of an adobe village, an adobe village as tall and expansive as a shining metropolis like New York City. While they traveled Aden told her what he knew about the city. "Callack city was built long before recorded history. Rock dragged from deep inside the earth and molded by some unknown extremely powerful wizards. Some say it was constructed by the gods themselves. Nobody is sure how they made the city. Somehow they reinforced the buildings and warded them against magic. That's why they could make the buildings so high but the spells that were used are long lost. Before Elysia was cut off from the rest of the world people came from every corner of the planet to visit Callack. I wish I could have seen the city 100 years ago before the troubles." "Troubles?" "Some say the gods left us. Whatever the cause Elysia is cut off from the rest of the world by deserts, mountains, cursed forest, and murderous races like the samebito. Now the city stagnates most of it is deserted but you don't want to hear about that." Tala listened and observed the citizens of Callack they wore clothing similar to that of people from the Renaissance fair back home but more sensible and with a modern twist. The people of Callack may not have had the technology of her world but over the centuries they had refined and mastered the art of making clothes by hand. Perhaps they had even incorporated magic in the process. She saw people shopping and kids playing in the alleys there were a few blacksmiths and trinket shops but the majority of the buildings were residential. Several hours later they arrived at the base of the mountain.

Words fail to describe the magnificence of what lay at the center of Callack. It was surely the most spectacular man made structure in this or any world. If it even was made by man. There was a large entrance built into the base that lead in to the hollow center of the mountain. Then a road spiraled up lining the inner wall of the mountain. The mountain itself had been altered to the point where it was no longer really a mountain. It had been shaven into a an almost perfect cylinder, then square holes had been carved straight though at 50 foot intervals creating what was essentially a ring of enormous square pillars. With horizontal rings connecting all the pillars every 50 feet. It was taller than any skyscraper that existed back home. The ring of columns supported the top of the mountain. Which seemed to be the only part of the mountain that remained solidly intact. The rings that connected the columns were met by the ascending spiral road that flattened at each level. To alleviate traffic there was another ascending road around the outside of the mountain. That ran parallel to the first and connected to the interior road in the spaces between the columns, allowing people to move freely back and forth at each level. The parts of the columns next to the spaces and level with the flat part of the road had each been carved out into its own little building. Making the mountain like an enourmous shopping mall where each floor has different stores above of the ones from the floor below. All of this was carved perfectly from the mountain. It was really a city in its own right.

 Aden and Tala crossed through the gate and began their assent up the inside of the mountain. Each new level they reached matched perfectly the previous level and yet was completely different. Each shop and dwelling had been made its own by the people that occupied it. After the shock of first beholding the mountain Aden told Tala about it. "The best and brightest of Callack are located here. In the mountain each level has a purpose." Aden explained "there's a level for the bankers, the law makers, army generals and strategists, and nobles. The scholars and historians work in the grand library on the top level just before the high ministry which is on top of the mountain. The grand library is also where all the wizards of Elysia are trained." "You are trained in a library." "Well it's got much more to it than your average library. It has hundreds of rooms and large chambers. Many the purpose for which has been long forgotten. But the bulk of them are taken up by books, articles, and various artifacts of knowledge, and it is in one of those parts that you will almost always find Issac." "This guy must be some sort of genius" "I might not go that far, but I always go to him whenever I need help."

It took them several more hours to reach the top level. The sun was down by the time they got there. However the interior of the mountain had become illuminated by something Tala was sure was magical. The last level was different from the others in the mountain. The road went through what she had thought was the roof and turned into a large circular courtyard that faced a grand entrance. Two long hallways went off to the right and left and curved out of sight. This whole part of the mountain was enclosed. The carriage stopped here and dropped them off. The driver announced he would be waiting for them in one of the stables on the levels beneath then descended leaving them in the crowded courtyard. Students, scholars, and a fair amount of civilians were hurriedly making their way to or from the entrance of the library. Aden ignored them and continued his tour guide speech. "The library is divided into three parts" Aden said "the dorms, the academy, and the main library. As I said I have a feeling he will be in the main library right in front, this way"

He started walking and lead her away they approached the entrance, a large doorway with two pillars on either side. Tala entered the library and again she marveled the main library was the size of a football stadium. At least 3 stories high with books and scrolls covering every inch of all the walls from floor to ceiling and countless bookshelves in between "how do you find anything" Tala asked. "magic" Aden said " it's part of a wizard scholar's job that's why they all live here in the grand library" "it is still a lot though isn't it" "they store all the knowledge and written history of Elysia in this library. You should probably stay with me so you don't get lost." "Isn't having everything here dangerous what if there is a fire you would lose everything.""Well there is a very special magic in this library that exists nowhere else in the world within these walls absolutely no harm can befall any person or object and the books are bewitched so they can't be removed from the library." "Wow, that's amazing. So where is this guy Issac." "I don't know let's find out."

Aden drew the attention of the man closest to themselves. He was a young man clearly a scholar of some sort. He wore glasses and was carrying a large stack of books. The one on the top was open and the man somehow managed to walk and read at the same time without running into anything. At first Tala did not think he would answer, but after a moment he raised his head. "Oh! Aden it's you, how can I help you" he said. "Yes thank you" Aden said "I was wondering if you could tell me where I could find Issac." "Oh yes of course" said the man "I believe he is in the geography section." "Forgive me I was never one for the library where is the geography section" Aden asked. The man sighed "you might get lost. Here you better let me show you. The man reached out with his pointer and middle finger and touched Aden on the forehead. There was a quick flash of light between the man's fingers and Aden's forehead and the man brought his hand back down. "Oh I see, thank you" said Aden. They shook hands "no thanks necessary it's my job and may I say it is good to see you back in Callack Aden." With that the man returned to his reading and walked away. "What did he do to you" Tala asked. "Most wizard scholars are users of magic dealing with the mind and perception. He placed a map in my mind that will guide me to Issac, come on."

Aden lead her towards the back of the library it took a while to get to the section of the library which housed the geography section. The books in this part of the library were old and dusty and there were few people there. This section of the library was clearly not popular, as they neared the geography section the people disappeared altogether, then they were upon it. The geography section was in the back left corner and made into its own room by a large bookshelf and an archway with a large word above it in a language she had never seen before. They entered, inside stood a man that Tala assumed was Issac because he was the only man in the room. He was staring at the wall in front of him very intently. He did not turn to them as they entered even though Tala was sure he must have noticed them. He was not as young as they were at least 30 he had spiked blond hair and was wearing baggy shorts the chain of a pocket watch hung on his leg the first sign of technology she had seen since arriving in Elysia he wore a thin white button down shirt and a gray silk vest that matched his slightly baggy shorts. Then his appearance began to drift from the norm as he appeared to have the legs and tail of a lion. However not like a centaur. He was still bipedal just with furry legs that ended in paws. They stood in silence for some time until Tala finally broke the silence "what is he." "Well that's kind of rude" the man said as he turned to them.

Issac smiled when he saw Aden. "It's been ages I'm sorry I didn't greet you right away. I thought you were my pesky apprentice again he gave Aden a big hug. "You really should give Aronica a break it's not her fault, you know how she is" said Aden. Issac broke the hug "so what do I owe the honor of your visit don't tell me you've decided to give up you foolish search and come back." Aden made a stern face then relaxed "Not at all she is why I'm here he pointed to Tala." "Oh hello miss I'm sorry I didn't realize you were a friend of Aden's, but you don't recognize an uridimmus when you see one. Well I guess I can't be too surprised we are quite rare these days." He took her hand and gave her a deep bow. "Anyways, my name is Issac". "Hi, I am Tala" she responded. "I was hoping you could help her" said Aden. "Sure anything what does she need" asked Issac. Aden flipped Tala's hood back revealing her elfin features Issac appeared to be struck dumb by the sight of her. After a few moments he regained his faculties and he hurriedly flipped her hood back on and looked around. "Aden do you know what this means! Come let's go someplace else more private. It's not safe here."

Issac took them to one of the hundreds of little reading nooks that dotted the library "why are you here are you an emissary, have the elves finally decided to break their silence" Issac asked her once he made doubly sure they could not be heard. "I don't know that's why we are here" she responded. "She doesn't seem to know anything about, well anything. We were hoping you could help her figure out who she is" Aden interrupted and gave Issac a look that communicated that she was not entirely to be trusted. "Oh" this seemed to trouble Issac. "Where did you find her" he asked. "In the slumbering wood near the river." "Well I may be able to help you but the information on you or your kind does not rest in my head. Come on let me show you something."

Issac took them and lead them to an area of the library that was completely accessible and yet so hidden in the rows of books you wouldn't be able to find it if you didn't know where it was. This new room was also filled with books maps and papers but it did not seem as organized as the rest of the library. Everything appeared handmade and excellently crafted. "This is the personnel library of the elves" Issac explained. "None of us at the library know the contents of anything in here we are sworn not to read anything. Even if we wanted to we can't it's all in the magical elvish language, which is undecipherable and impossible to learn. Only elves can speak or write it but you Tala you're an elf. You will be able to read the texts. They may hold the answers you seek." "Okay, I don't know if I can but I'll try reading it" she said. "Good I suggest you start there" Issac pointed to a very, very large book in the middle of the room. "That is where the recorded history of elves was kept" Issac told her. "Check the last entry Tala." She went to the book the writing in the book consisted of strange symbols she had never seen before and yet somehow she understood them perfectly. It was the oddest sensation she had ever felt. Instantly understanding an entire language she had no knowledge of before but for the thousandth time since she arrived in Elysia she forced herself to shake off her disbelief, concentrate, and read the final entry on the last page. Hoping she would get some answers. "Okay" she said to Issac and Aden "I can read it but, all it says is."

> "Praise the goddess, she has many
> arms reaching outstretched,
> rest in them and you will be safe"

"A prayer" said Aden "that's weird. Isn't that supposed to be a history book why would there be religion in there?" "The elves are closer to their god than any other species, but a prayer doesn't help us. Try going back a page does it say anything else?" asked Issac. "No" replied Tala "nothing." "Well then I suspect it might not a prayer at all but some sort of riddle. The elves are famous for them and they are often poetic, but what does it mean." Issac went quiet for a while. Several minutes later he said "it is telling you to go to Ælfwynn forest" "what makes you so sure" asked Aden clearly distressed. "The elven goddess is Ælfwynn and elves live in the forest of course but the arm line is what sold it. I've seen depictions of Ælfwynn she only has two arms but trees have many arms and forests have many more. Ælfwynn forest is named after the goddess of the elves. It's not meant to be a difficult riddle to solve its meant as a message" said Issac. "But we don't know if the message is meant for Tala, besides its suicide to enter the forest, the elves live there they turned against us long ago" said Aden. "What are you talking about" said Tala.

Aden sighed "I knew we would have to discuss this eventually. The truth is the reason seeing you, an elf, is such a big deal is because elves have killed everyone that has managed to see them for the last hundred years. Ælfwynn forest is known by another name, the cursed wood." "So we are evil" said Tala. "That is a good question." "Then how can you trust me." "How indeed" said Issac. There was a tense silence between them Aden was the first to break it. "Isn't there anymore information here, we are the first ones in here in almost 100 years there must be more." Issac responded "there won't be any more useful information here. This riddle was the last message left behind to help any elves that needed guidance. If you wanna know more about her you will ask to ask an elf. I wouldn't be so worried. I have a feeling that if you take an elf into the forest you will be okay." "Arrgh! This is so frustrating" said Tala "I just want to know why I am here." "She's right Issac there has to be more here" "I don't think there is Aden but you have all the time you need to look." Just then there was a thunderous crack and an explosion that sent fire into the library it filled every crack and crevice inside and all three of them erupted in flame.

Tala started to panic for a moment then she realized she was fine. She did not understand what was happening until she remembered the enchantment on the library that protected everything inside it. A few moments later the flames receded. "What was that" said Aden. "I'm not sure, we better check it out" Issac responded. They ran to the front of the library to see what was going on but all they saw was the end of a huge spiked scaly tail sliding out of a now completely destroyed front entrance of the library, and the stunned faces of all the library patrons. Aden ran up to one of the folk at the front of the library "what was that" he asked. The horrified man shakingly let out a stream of words "it was a   dra,dra,dra dragon it took the head minister." "What no!" Issac yelled and bolted for the door. Aden and Tala ran after him. "it doesn't make any sense" said Aden why would a dragon be here unless....." he trailed off lost in thought. A minute later they made it out onto the street where all three of them froze midstep. They stared in horror at the destruction outside of the library. A third of the buildings all the way down the mountain were engulfed in flames. Like a giant birthday cake. There were people running and screaming all around some were okay, most were not as lucky, they flailed around on fire or worse. but that was not what made them freeze. That was not the main threat.

All around them people were being beset upon by hundreds of winged beings in light armor. They carried large flaming swords and they flew about slaughtering everyone in sight, setting fire to everything else. "What the hell are those?" Aden gasped "they're not harpies" .Tala finally knew something that Aden didn't. "Those are angels" she said. "No it can't be proclaimed Issac. "There hasn't been an angel in Elysia since the age of the gods, how do you even know what they look like?" "Angels are prominent in the place I come from due to religion. They are in all kinds of art and literature. I'm not very religious but I would recognize one anywhere. Does this mean we are being attacked by god?" "Just forget them where is the dragon?" said Aden. "They all looked around trying to gaze though the chaos finally Issac pointed to a spot in the sky right next to the mountain. "There" he said.

Off to the side of the mountain hovered a large black reptile twice the size of a bus. There it was slowly flapping its large leathery wings as it finished eating what appeared to be the rest of the head minister. A young man no older then Aden but with an evil look on his face that made him appear ancient sat on the back of the dark dragon commanding the angels. "Raven!" Aden cried and in sheer fury. As he screamed his entire body burst into a flame so intense Tala felt like she was on fire even though she was standing 3 yards away. It appeared to be too hot even for Brand who turned to ash. "I'll kill you, you bastard!" Aden screamed but before he could move in a flash the mind wizard Issac spun in front of him, placing his middle and pointer finger on to Aden's forehead. "What?...no!" were all the words Aden had time to say before his flames went out and he lost consciousness.

Issac caught him as he fell. "Tala" he called "come here there's no time to explain you've got to promise me that you'll take him out of the city if he stays here he'll die." "What about you" she asked "I have to stay here and hold them off don't worry I will be okay." Tala could tell by the way he talked there was no arguing with him or maybe that was just her fear talking. Either way she agreed. "Okay I promise" she said. Issac gently handed Aden to Tala. She took Aden from Issac and draped him over her shoulders with her new elfin strength she could easily carry him on her shoulder. "But how will you fight you have no weapon. He took the watch out of his pocket and it instantly melted and transformed into a large broadsword "how." "Simple transmutation" he interrupted "now quickly you must go there isn't much time goe to Ælfwynn forest it's your best hope, that way" he pointed west. "Travel though the abandoned parts of the city he will awaken in 4 days. You'll be well on your way by the time he wakes up now quickly please." "Alright I'll do it" she ran off down the outer mountain road. Issac marveled at how carrying the considerable bulk of Aden did not seem to slow the elf. "Amazing "he said then he turned back to the chaos just in time to deflect a flaming sword aimed at his head.

Tala ran down to the winding road to the base of the mountain carrying Aden and dodging panicked pedestrians and killer angels, but it wasn't long before the spectacle of an elf woman sprinting though the streets carrying a man attracted attention. Several angels, three of them broke off from the pack and came after her. She ducked the first angel's swing and came around drawing her sword. Tala's skill with a blade had increased exponentially since her fight with the strix. However the angels were clearly much stronger and they were skilled in swordplay. Tala fought valiantly and even managed to dispatch an angel with a stab to the chest, but the others where to skilled and the burden of carrying Aden slowed her down they pushed her back to her left.

More angels broke away from the pack and closed in on her, she looked around franticly for an escape route but she was still 100 feet up the mountain and the way down was blocked. Then she saw it here way out a nearby rooftop just within jumping distance. She broke off from the group and bolted for the edge of the road. An angel moved in front of her blocking off her escape route but Tala quickly side stepped, spun around behind him and shoved him. Sending the angel colliding into the group of angels that had been pursuing her. During the moments it took them to recover and take chase she covered the remaining distance to the ledge and without a second thought leaped to the nearby roof.

As soon as she landed safely with Aden still on her back she bolted across the tan stone roof, with the angels still hot on her tail. When she reached the end of the roof she leaped to the next rooftop about ten feet below then jogged for the next rooftop. After that picking up speed. Tala bounded from building to building running faster than a horse. By the time she reached the fifth building she was starting to leave the angels behind. It looked like she was gonna escape them. Tala couldn't believe it, that's when she heard an earth shattering roar from behind her. Tala did not have to look behind her to know she had attracted the attention of the dragon and its rider. For nothing else could have produced such a magnificent roar, however she looked all the same. The monster was on her tail and gaining fast. His scales so black he covered the whole sky with darkness. Making it seem like night was coming wherever it flew, and the beast was currently casting its huge formidable shadow on Tala. By the time Tala had jumped the next 2 roofs the dragon had closed half of the distance between them. Tala again seeked a way to escape a fight she knew she could not win, but Tala was still a good 40 feet off the ground. There was no place to run. So she concentrated and pushed her new body to its limits. Tala approached unnatural speeds she ran faster than the wind and leaped 20 feet with each bound. She did not lose the dragon but she did eventually prevent it from gaining on her. Unfortunately the strain was enormous. Her tendons started to rip and tear and still she ran but she could not keep it up forever. It was only a matter of time.

Raz watched the angelic genocide with bloodlust. He longed to join the slaughter. Even for a dragon he was particularly ruthless. He ached to join the fight but his master held him back. He was forced to be content with eating one fat old human. What did he care if he was some fancy high minister, he did not make a good meal. Even for a human he was bland and chewy. Then to Raz's delight his master gave him the signal to pursue a woman already being chased by a group of angels and carrying a man on her back. He immediately sprung into action intent on beating the angels to the prize. The dragon did not understand why his master would care about a single woman but was eager for action and jumped at the opportunity. As Raz followed her he knew there was something strange about her. The woman ran much faster than any human should be able to. Even with his speed and determination he had trouble keeping up with her let alone catching her. Furthermore the woman had a strange scent. It was familiar yet he could not put his claw on where in his past he had smelled it. Raz started to tire he could not keep up this speed for much longer. His master gave him the signal to end the chase sensing the dragon's fatigue.

While Raz always liked to be sporting during a hunt he dare not disobey his master. So instead the dragon inhaled and blew a huge plume of liquid fire from deep within his chest and blasted the roof in front of the girl. The fire hit its target reducing a large portion of the roof to slag. The woman tried to stop she dug her heels deep into the roof but she was moving much too fast and eventually the force of her momentum overturned her body and she tumbled into the building. The dragon spread his wings to their full extension and slowed the beats landing gracefully on the roof. Raz peered into the building it appeared to be a huge pit even with his eagle like eyesight Raz could not see the bottom. The floors of the building must have collapsed from age or perhaps his attack had done it. Whatever the cause it surely meant the women had fallen to her death but Raz had to make sure his prey was dead. The dragon belched another blast of fire into the hole. The jet raced through the building blasting though all the windows as it surged to the bottom of the structure. Raz continued to unleash his murderous breath into the pit for several seconds before he stopped. Satisfied his master signaled the dragon to return to the chaos back at the mountain and Raz turned to leave. Before he left Raz was reminded of what the woman was as he inhaled a scent much stronger and more familiar than what he had gotten earlier the smell of burning elf flesh.

Bella awoke again in a dark dank cell something she was familiar with as a werewolf but this time it stung a little more emotionally than usual. She felt like she had been asleep for days. Bella looked at the surrounding prison. It was definitely underground some sort of dungeon. It stank of fear, waste, and death. Bella felt a weird sensation in her feet and looked down to see a rat nibbling on her toe. She growled and kicked her foot flinging the rat into the corner. It slid down the wall, then righted its self and returned to the shadows but not before looking at her as if to say "I'll be back." She felt at her chest and to her relief found that her lunar pendant was still there. She was surprised that the strange trinket meant so much to her since she had just got it. She knew it shouldn't but it still did. "That's a pretty necklace"

Bella stiffened "don't be scared. I'm a friend at least I think I am" said a man from the cell next to her. He was well dressed but his clothes were torn and dirty he was not young but he wasn't old maybe early 30s and he smiled as he looked at her. "Well that's an awfully creepy thing for a friend to say especially from an old guy in a dungeon. Anyway if you're really my friend tell me. How'd I get here and where is here" Bella asked her strange new companion. "I don't know how you got here. You were already here when I arrived. I just got here and I'm sorry I assure you I didn't mean to sound creepy and old as you so kindly put it. Let's have a fresh start my name is Issac. What's yours?" Bella eyed him carefully " Issac huh funny I was just on my way to see an Issac when I was captured, but it was probably someone else and I think he would have mentioned you were an uridimmus. Issac is a common enough name. Either way my name is Bella. So do you at least know where we are then?"

"Yes I do, but it's not good. We are in shadow city in the dungeon of the dark castle itself as a matter of fact." "The shadow city" said Bella "why are we here." "Well I don't know why you're here but I was captured during the attack on Callack city. It was terrible the only reason I'm alive is because I know a significant amount of things that their leader wants to know. "There was an attack on Callack city?" asked Bella in a nervous voice. "I am afraid so, it came out of nowhere a tragedy many of the people there were killed, slaughtered by a man named Raven commanding an angel army." "Oh no! my friends and I were on the way to Callack city when I was taken. I hope they are okay." "Well I don't want to upset you, I did managed to get most of the survivors in to the library for protection but it was too little too late. If they were in the city I think it's best if you don't get your hopes up. This is a tragedy that surely will not be equaled for centuries." Issac watched as the girl stared of into space deep in thought "it must be hard for you being so young. That is a nice necklace though" he said "yes very interesting"

Tala woke up and was greeted by an extreme pain like she had never felt before in her life. She was lying in a heap at the bottom of the building she had fallen into. She had survived by somehow managing to conjure up foliage beneath her to cushion the fall but it was not enough to fully absorb the impact from the 40 foot free fall. She estimated she had several broken ribs and a broken arm but that was nothing compared to the Burns.

The dragon had left her with severe burns that stretched from her chest to her stomach and down her left leg the very air stung. Tala did not know much about medicine but she knew her life was in danger. Even if she managed to survive the pain and avoid infection there would be permanent scaring. She struggled to turn her head and look at Aden. She was glad to see he was much better off than she was. He didn't appear to have broken anything in the fall but she wouldn't know until he was awake. He had no burns at all, Tala wondered how that was possible then she remembered how Aden had burst into flame when he had seen the man on the mountain. It occurred to her he was probably fireproof. Still in a daze, she examined her surroundings. Tala was in a dark room at the bottom of one of the many abandoned buildings in Callack. There was stone rubble and dust all around her she could clearly see the holes in the ceilings above her where she had fallen through right up to the sky. Then she remembered about her pursuers she had to get up. Tala reined in her senses and focused her mind pushing the pain to the back of her consciousness. Tala tried to sit up her body's response was immediate. After the enormous surge off pain hit her she realized she had made a mistake and fell back to the ground she laid there on the verge of losing consciousness.

Finally she burst into tears as much from pain as from a feeling of sheer hopelessness. She continued to cry honestly hoping for the first time since coming there she was home. Adventure wasn't fun anymore. There was often a time in the books when the hero was in her situation but he was always able to get up. No matter how much blood they had lost they persevered through sheer power of will. Now she knew it was all bullshit. No amount of willpower was getting her up Tala knew now why there were so few heroes in real life, heroes die. So realizing all this Tala cried she cried and cried until the pain finally made her drift off into unconsciousness.

Tala woke up sometime the following day. This time she was a lot more careful about how much she moved. She checked her surroundings and surmised it was sometime around noon. Tala checked her wounds she was surprised to see they had already started healing. Tala's pain had also lessened to a degree. Tala remained wary of trying to move however remembering her previous experience. So she just laid there, she remained still for a long time thinking about her next move. Finally she decided she should just go for it and tried to sit up which she accomplished fairly easily. The pain did spark but it was manageable. This time she remained conscious. The fact that she was still alive meant that her attacker had obviously presumed her dead. She looked over at Aden he still looked fine. She on the other hand was feeling very thirsty her lips were cracked and screaming for water and her stomach growled.

Seemingly responding to her thoughts the plants she had landed on suddenly burst into life and produced a single large ripe piece of fruit. She ignored how bizarre the miracle was taking it in stride at this point, she graciously ate it .When Tala had finished the fruit she decided to push herself even more and stood up. The terrible pain from her burns surged with each new motion however Tala continued to deal with the pain. She sighed then carefully moved over to Aden and checked him for wounds. Upon closer inspection Aden still didn't seem to have any broken bones.

"Lucky you" she thought feeling the pain from her ribs, and then she realized she should probably put a splint on her arm. She looked around to no avail. The room she was in was bare stripped of everything by its previous owners but again her miracle plant gave her the solution. One of its branches stiffened, became hardwood, then fell to the floor. The magical splint had even grown vines from the sides so she could easily secure it to her arm. After she finished tying the branch to her arm she made sure one more time Aden was okay. Then with great effort slowly walked out onto the street. There was no one in sight, not surprising since this was an abandoned part of the city but something told Tala that the rest of the city was probably just as quiet. Then a chill went through her accompanied by a stinging pain as the wind blew down the cobblestone streets of the tan colored city. It was awfully quiet in Callack that day the only sign of life was a pillar of smoke rising from the center of the city.

****

"Raven!" Aden cried as he awoke. For a while he was stunned, out of sorts from being unconscious for so long but over time he began to remember what had happened. "Issac why did he stop me and Raven how could he go so far as to attack Callack was he even human anymore had he ever been?" Aden sat up "oh good you are awake!" he looked over to find Tala staring back at him clearly worried "what happened where are we" he asked. "Well were somewhere on the way to Ælfwynn forest and well I was kind of hoping you would tell me what happened." It was then that Aden noticed the burns along her body and the splint on her arm and that he himself felt much bruised to say the least. "How did you get hurt" asked Aden. Tala sighed "when I ran away that man and the dragon chased us and we fell into one of the abandoned buildings. To be honest I think we were lucky to get away at all. I wonder how many of the people in Callack could say that." "Well your wounds do seem to be healing okay that's one good thing." Tala found herself very happy that Aden cared so much about her.

"Here" she said have some fruit she handed him one of the pieces of fruit Tala had picked off the magic plant before she left. You must be starving I was able to give you water while you were out but you haven't eaten anything in a while." She was right Aden hadn't been this hungry since he had gotten lost in the Monde dessert on an expedition his first year of training. He had almost died, but the experience gave him much more knowledge than his classmates got. Aden eagerly took the fruit and began eating. "How long was I out we gotta get back" Aden said quickly between bites. "I was starting to get worried Issac said you would be out for 4 days" " I've been out for four days!" "no, not exactly" "Good was going to lose my mind" "um, it's been a week" "a week! Raven was back there who knows what's happened" "Issac told said if we had stayed you would have died and I have to agree you saw what was back there." " That is not for you to decide you have know idea what raven has done what he will do if I do not…" Aden started to argue when his stomach rumbled and he looked as if he might faint. "dammit I'm still too hungry to argue right now. It was just then that he noticed that there was a large stag grazing just to the right of him no more than 4 meters away. Delighted at the prospect of meat but too weak to hunt he prepared a spell to slay the beast that would also do a fairly decent job of cooking it in the process. He gathered the magical energy and brought up his right hand which slowly began to glow red hot. The spell came easy he had fully recovered his magical energy during his rest he had never felt this replenished. When he had finished collecting the energy for the spell in his hand he threw it up at the animal. Tala moving at an inhuman speed grabbed his hand and magically dispersed the energy.

"wait no don't !" he is a friend he found me outside of Callack and helped me carry you here as long as I promised not to eat any more of his kind. His name is Woodrush." Aden looked at her and slowly lowered his arm. Alerted by the noise and the movement the stag looked up at them then, he determined that nothing of interest was going on and returned to his grazing. "You can talk to him then" Aden queried Tala. "Well not exactly, it's more like we just kind of understand each other." "Uh huh ... and where did you learn to disperse magical energy?" "I'm not sure lately I've just kind of been doing things." "And that didn't strike you as odd." "Well yeah but so does everything I figured it was pretty run of the mill for this place." "Amazing" Aden thought "this kind of increase of strength when not only a week ago you had not even found your magic. It is unheard of it usually takes wizards years to master such a skill. Then there's that stag he looked over at the deer and examined it. On closer inspection he realized it was huge larger than a horse even the size of a moose. He had assumed that it was impossible for a deer to be that large and perceived it to be much closer than it was but even from such a distance he could sense the magic oozing from him a sign that it was a magical animal.

"A familiar" he said out loud. "What?" Tala asked "it's a white hart a magical deer that leads heroes to adventure. It must be your familiar. You really didn't know?" Aden responded then went back to eating fruit. Tala stared at him clearly wanting to say something. "what?" he asked "well what was that back there you knew that man what's going on" Aden finished his fruit while he listened to her when she was finished asking her question he was quiet for a minute then let out a chuckle. "you know it's funny I know not to trust you but my gut keeps telling me I should" Tala looked at him confused "what are you talking about?" Aden ignored her and continued to speak seeming to be more mumbling to himself than talking to her "I mean you are obviously a spy" "Aden what are you talking about" Tala pleaded with him but he just keep going "you show up out of nowhere just days before the attack. What are the odds the first elf in almost a century shows up right next to my camp needing my help. A defenseless elf claiming she knew nothing of magic or weapons. Says she's not from Elysia not even from this world, and I'm supposed to believe it's not related." He turned to Tala his temper flaring no longer able to suppress his suspicion "that you know what angels are, read elvish but your knot from Elysia the birthplace and only home of elves! And that you didn't know about Raven or the attack how stupid do you think I am! You were obviously sent here to spy on me who sent you! The elves or was it Raven himself?" Tala said nothing she just stood frozen in shock tears welling up in her eyes "well answer me!" Tala managed to speak "Aden how could you think that, are you saying this was all an act I thought you cared" "stop treating me like an idiot you elves have been killing every human that has gone in that forest for 100 years why, why should I trust you!" suddenly Tala's world was unraveling she could no longer put on a brave face she broke down "because I need you! I thought this was what I wanted. An adventure in a strange fantastic new land but all this death this pain. Not knowing where I am how to get home I'm scared. I just want it to stop and I need you. Through this whole thing you've been there your all I have please stop this!" her words where barely audible though the gasping and tears Tala turned his back to him while she cried.

Aden's face softened as he looked at her, her burns just visible from her side. He realized the only one being dishonest here was him with himself. His own pain and anger had been the real cause of his outburst. There was no doubt in his heart that he could trust her completely. She had cared for him and carried him this far even though she herself was more injured than him .what he was sure of above all else was that he couldn't let her continue to suffer. He kneeled next to Tala and wrapped his arms around her she quieted down and looked at him but continued to cry

"I'm sorry" he said "you know my feelings have never lead me astray. One time I ignored them and it was the biggest mistake in my life. From then on I swore never to do it again. I trust my feelings more than any magic and right now they are telling me I am an idiot for not believing you and for making you cry. They are also telling me to trust you with all my heart. So I will, do you forgive me." Tala brushed away her tears "do you promise not to leave me?" " I promise." "Wow, I am so weak why did I do that" Tala said. "Let me tell you something, during the time I spent with you, I have faced more trials than I have my entire life. The fact you are taking it so well with no experience is amazing. I would be dead without you so give yourself more credit. Really, who needs who?" Tala smiled "I guess."

"You were right before. You need to know what's happening but to tell you I need to start from the beginning. Sit down it's a long tale I'm about to tell. They took a minute to cool down after their heated discussion. Tala's deer had hovered over them ever since. Clearly disapproving of Aden's presence, Tala keep him from attacking but the beast glared and tiny flower buds on his antlers rapidly bloomed and receded, in what had to be the prettiest display of anger imaginable. Aden cautiously eyed the deer while he ate another piece of fruit and mourned when it finally sunk in that he might never have a chance to talk to Issac again because he and so many of the other citizens of callack were probably dead. When Tala was seated comfortably across from him and started to look impatient he began speaking.

Aden's Story

I was born in Pakarr village and when I was young I lived a simple life. I laughed and played with the local children. All I dreamed of was to one day be a farmer like my father. It was just my father and I at that time. My mother died soon after I was born. But my father and I made a good life together. Then when I was 5 a boy stumbled into town from the woods. Like you he knew nothing of this world. Most of the villagers thought he was crazy and likely a werewolf. They rejected him forcing him to beg on the streets. My father took pity on the boy and invited him into our home. He was the same age as I was and soon we grew to be the closest of friends, inseparable. I considered him my brother. The three of us together could not be a happier family, but then a little after my tenth birthday my father grew ill nobody knew why. The healers in our village were just wise men not wizards they couldn't help. The village council sent word to Callack asking for a healer of the magical type. That was when I met master Kroft .He was a great sorcerer, far too educated and powerful to respond to such a simple call for a healer. However the call was urgent and he was close by doing some research. He was only 2 days away but those two days were two days to many, my father past away shortly after the call for a healer went out.

I was stricken with grief. My brother as I had grown to call him had not known my father as long, but I knew it hit him as hard as it hit me. However in my time of sorrow my brother stayed strong he consoled me and helped me though the pain. When master Kroft arrived in town he found us alone and grieving. He saw that we had magic in us and took us on as apprentices. No the better phrase is he adopted us. He moved to Pakarr and trained us personally. I can't tell you what kind of honor that was it is almost unheard of for such a high ranking wizard to work so closely with a wizard though their entire training. When he told us of his intent to train us we had mixed feelings.

It was a great opportunity to become a wizard but in our village wizards were seen as somewhat eccentric and untrustworthy. However we longed for someone to look after us in the absence of my father so we agreed. My brother took to it much better than I did within a week he had discovered his magic. It took me quite a while longer but after a lot of meditating I found it. I wanted to be a healer more than anything. So that I could save people like my father, but when I attempted healing magic I completely failed. Master Kroft said that we do not get to choose what kind of wizard we are destiny choses for us. He said in order to find out what you are destined for you have to look deep within yourself to discover the true nature of your magic. It was like that I discovered my inner flame. However this made me very depressed fire wizards were not known to help people only wage war and destroy. I rejected my magic and resolved not to use it again. In my sorrow my brother came to me and he showed me my powers could be used for good. Those were great times, happy times. Just the three of us a family again but a little after my 14th birthday everything changed.

One night on a full moon I had a strange feeling urging me, telling me my brother was in danger, but I didn't listen. I ignored it and went to sleep. When I awoke the next morning my brother was missing and he stayed missing for a week. We looked everywhere, searched the whole forest twice and then some, but we never found him. I began to fear the worst but we never found a body. There was talk in town he had been eaten by werewolves. Then on the seventh night I awoke to find master Kroft was gone. I knew something was wrong and ran straight into the woods I knew he was there. I can't explain it but I knew exactly where he was. I ran and ran into a deep dark long forgotten part of the woods. One I could not have found before that night if I looked 1000 years. When I finally found the entrance to the dark cave that I knew my master was in, several hours had past. The cave was dark and smelled like death I wanted nothing more than to not go into that cave, but for my master I would do anything.

I entered the cave, after walking a bit the dark rugged walls and floor of the cave turned in to soft smooth sandstone. Every inch of the ceiling floor and walls was inscribed with hieroglyphics. I stopped to examine them, but I could make no sense of the writing, so I continued on. The walls narrowed into a hallway. Then a narrow shaft that descended steadily into the earth. Every minute felt like an eternity as I descended the shaft. Then finally the shaft opened up into a large chamber mostly occupied by a very large statue of a dark god named Democles. I knew him from illustrations in books I looked around the chamber searching for my master. To my horror I found him crumpled up lying on an alter at the foot of the statue. I ran to him as fast as I could but in my heart I knew it would do no good. When I got to the alter I saw what I feared I would see. There was a gaping wound in his gut. The attacker had cut him and left him to die. However there was hope the wound itself was not fatal as long as you stopped the bleeding in time. I knew this as I had read every medical book I could get my hands on.

So I summoned my powers and carefully cauterized the wound the closest thing to healing I could perform. Then I stepped back and waited. A few moments later my master awoke I was already at his side by the time his lids were half open. "Are you all right" I asked. He didn't answer at first, when he did it was in a low raspy voice and his breathing was labored. "I am okay, but I am also going to die very soon." I said "what kind of talk is that. Dying is not okay you'll be alright I've healed your wound." He said "you did a good job Aden I'm proud of you but I've lost too much blood. It's just a matter of time. Do not be sad for me I've lived longer than most men it's just my time." I cried "how can you say that you were attacked tell me who did this to you." "If I tell you do you promise not to seek vengeance?" I would have promised anything. "Sure master I promise" I said. "Ok then I'll tell you but only because he needs you. It was Raven he did it but he is not to blame. Please you must not hurt him he needs your help." I agreed I said "ok master if that is your wish I will respect it." He said "good then I can die in peace." I didn't get it how could there be peace after this, and then he said "but before I go I must tell you one thing. There was a saying at the academy when I was a child. The only difference between men and gods is a little magic. It is true that after this you must face Raven but I plead with you when you do don't fight him if you do he'll kill you. Remember there is always another way" and with that he closed his eyes, and that was the last I saw of my master, or my brother Raven.

The truth was that I had lied to my master. I could not keep the promise I made to him. If it was anyone else a bandit or a lunatic I might have been able to, but my own brother. That is a betrayal I could not, cannot forgive. My master tried to stop me because he thought I was too weak. So I joined the academy worked restlessly and graduated 4 years early at the top of my class. After that I hunted my brother for over a year, but I found no trace of him none at all, until he attacked Callack. I even went back to look in the cave for clues, but I couldn't find it. It was like it had vanished, and then I found you. The only places I haven't looked for him are Ælfwynn forest and shadow city. That's why I agreed to go to the forest I thought if I had an elf with me I would be granted safe passage. You see then I thought Raven was just a man like me and could be hiding anywhere, but that thing on the dragon was no man it was a monster. It was evil, and it was my brother its name is Raven. I know now I can feel it in my stomach. I guess deep down I've always known. I just didn't want to admit he was that far gone. I know where I need to go and evil like that can't hide. I know he's not in the forest he's in shadow city were evil thrives."

Aden finished his story and Tala could see the pain on his face. She absorbed the information she had heard before speaking "Well now I know why Issac knocked you out." "What?" he said. "You have to stop what you're doing Raven must be stopped but not for revenge. Revenge stories never end well, trust me. He needs to be stopped because it's what's right. If you fight for any other reason you'll lose. You said you have such a good intuition, so listen to it. What does your heart tell you to do"Tala said and slapped a hand to her chest. Aden sighed "you are right, but for the first time in my life I just don't know what to do." "It's okay Aden just calm down you just came to. I understand why you're so upset but maybe things will be clearer if you just relax for a while." "Thanks Tala maybe your right let's just slow things down and think."

Suddenly a cry issued from deeper in the woods. Followed suddenly by large vines that crawled across the ground and rapped around their legs, even the white hart was entangled. As they were attacked by the vines Aden realized that Tala had brought them within the boundaries of the forest. In all the excitement before he hadn't noticed. Aden looked back down at his feet the vines continued to climb up his body encasing him in a shell of plant life. "Are you okay Tala!" Aden yelled to her as he struggled against the vines, and cursed himself for not noticing their dangerous surroundings sooner. "Not great!"She yelled. Aden could only see her out of the corner of his eye because the vines had climbed high enough to restrict the movement of his head. He continued to struggle against the vines to no avail; just as the vines were about to cover his eyes and Aden thought all hope was lost. He saw a flash, and heard Tala's body hit the ground. Then the vines finished encasing him, and all he could see was darkness.

A few moments later he heard Tala's muffled voice penetrate the darkness "are you okay in there." The vines held him so tight Aden could not move his mouth to answer her. "Hold on I'll have you out in a minute", Aden felt the pressure on his shoulder where Tala was trying to cut though the vines. She was progressing steadily and was almost though the vines when Aden heard Tala's voice again. "who are you, what do you want, we don't want to hurt you, wait stop let him go, no get off me, look I'm an elf like you." Her cries were accompanied by other voices talking in a language that Aden didn't recognize, and the clatter of a violent struggle. After a few seconds the struggling stopped, and Tala's voice slowly faded into the distance. Everything was quiet for a while, and Aden feared

Tala had been captured or worse. Aden couldn't breathe well in the cocoon and his mind started to fog. Finally the silence was broken by a slithering noise as the vines slowly released Aden, and he fell to the ground arms on fire, ready to fight in an instant.

When he looked up he saw an angry looking group of elves holding Tala and the white hart with swords at their necks, and one of them had his hand over Tala's mouth. Aden's temper flared, and so did his flames, as he thought about attacking. However, reason prevailed. Slowly he dropped his arms, and let his flames go out. "What do you want" Aden asked, looking as defeated as he felt. The elves spoke something in their strange language that sounded more like the rustling of leaves and the babbling of a brook than actual words. "I don't understand you" Aden said, the elf who had spoken stepped forward and spoke again, this time in common tongue "I said stand down and come with us or the girl dies."

Aden stared away thoughtfully for a moment then spoke "where are you going to take us" he asked. "To our leader" the elf spoke without hesitation, there was a moment of tension as Aden thought about the situation, and the elves looked ready to pounce if he so much as twitched. Finally he relented and let the elves bind his hands, and lead him away. The small procession walked quickly and quietly, though the forest, though Tala was definitely trying to break the silence. She made angry faces and tried to scream though the gag, they had put on her "just let her talk it can't hurt, you've already caught us". "We can't" said the elf that talked using common tongue. "Why not" Aden demanded, "orders" replied the elf. After several hours of walking though the uneven forest terrain Aden began to tire, "where are we going" "Ælfwynn" responded the elf. "We're already in Ælfwynn, what are you talking about." "I tire of your mouth human, we could gag you too." Aden decided to be quiet and just bide his time; he looked to the back of the pack and saw the white hart following the procession, he was keeping his distance but looked like he desperately wanted to attack the elves. He knew better though so like Aden he just followed.

Aden counted eight elves making up the group that had abducted them, they were probably all magic users, most elves were, he would have no chance in a straight up fight against them. "Brand!" he thought "he can help, I just have to summon him, all I need is some ash." Aden looked around and immediately realized his folly. He should have known better then to expect to find ash in a forest and he supply had been separated from him at some point. Aden gave up on escaping for the moment, "well we wanted to find the elves" he thought "so let's just see what happens."

It took them three hours to get to the elf village. Tala knew because she had been counting every second. She had little else to do during the walk, because the whole way there, they had muzzled her. A fact made more annoying because they did not silence Aden, nor did they escort him. They just let him walk with the group while Tala was flanked by warriors. Tala had understood everything the elves had said, but it gave her little insight. All they said to one another were instructions and things like that. Get this, I'm over here, shut him up, don't be so ruff, take them around here, pass around water, nothing of significance.

As they entered the village Tala looked around, there were very few elves around, the place seemed almost deserted. The elves that were there moved soundlessly, and never spoke. They were all just as beautiful as Tala with perfect features. They all looked very similar as if everyone in the village were close relatives. The elve's homes where just as beautiful as they were. More like the houses of her world than those in Callack, but less advanced and more extravagant. Like villas in the woods. They were built in the trees and they were all built in an ascending spiral pattern, with one long continuous house wrapping up and around each tree. There appeared to be several families living in each tree at the different levels. Their homes were interconnected by a huge web of rope bridges and wooden cat walks on each level that attached to the patios of the homes, and lead up or down in a kind of multilevel neighborhood. Tala was enchanted, she had never seen anything more beautiful. It made her feel like she could stay there forever.

Tala snapped back to reality when they began approaching a large tree in the center of the village. This tree was different from all the others unlike the other trees with houses built on the outside, this tree was massive, and it appeared to be hollow. There were perfectly shaped windows cut from the tree every couple of yards. It looked to Tala like a giant skyscraper of living wood. The only part of the tree that didn't have windows cut from it was a large section in the exact middle of the tree. Located there was the most spectacular feature of the living tree. Facing Tala from the middle of the tree was a very large and extravagant carving of an elf woman. Her beauty was so great that it was almost tangible. Her hair flowed out in all directions over the trunk, and she wore a long elegant dress that billowed eternally in some nonexistent wind. Tala could not imagine the amount of time and effort that must have gone in to making something like that. The carving was amazingly pristine, the visage was godlike, and yet it seemed very comforting to Tala. As if she was looking at a friend. There was something very familiar about the woman carved into the tree, but she could not put her finger on why. Tala noticed there were no bridges leading to this tree it was isolated, alone, strong, and stoic.

Tala continued to stare at the figure as they entered the tree.

Inside the tree there were even fewer elves than in the sparsely populated village. All the elves here had a different appearance then those she had seen thus far. They all appeared ancient, they were tall and pale with long thinning hair some even had beards which appeared non-existent in the other elves she had seen so far. To match their skin and hair they all wore long white robes while the other elves appeared to prefer green. Unlike the elves in the town which had occasionally looked at the procession to see what was going on. These elves did not look away from their work. They were definitely not ordinary civilians, one look at them told you they were the leaders of this village. The elves that were escorting her did not bring them to one of the elders like she had expected but took her deeper into the tree higher and higher they climbed until they reached a large chamber in the tree with no windows and yet it was illuminated by some magical witch light.

Tala suspected they were directly behind the large carving of the woman on the outside of the tree and as if to confirm her suspicions there was a large human sized wooden statue of the women in the middle of the chamber that exactly matched the one outside. The elves brought them to stand right in front of the statue then they released Tala. She took no time to catch her breath before she began screaming at the elves. "Who do you think you are gaging me like that, what kind of people are you?" The elves remained silent for a while Tala's scolding seemed to make them very uneasy. Finally the elf in charge dropped to one knee and the other elves immediately followed. He spoke I am very sorry milady. We could not allow you to speak." "Why" Tala demanded clearly confused but still mad. "If you had told us to do something we would be honor bound to do so. We have all sworn oaths of fealty to serve you, but we had orders to bring you here and could not risk you refusing. Just know you have my deepest apologies and that it pained me greatly to have you bound like that." "I don't understand I've never even met you how could you have sworn fealty to me." "We may not have met but all the elves know who you are you're the 1st princess of the realm of elves Tala Ælfwynn. Formally Tala brown of earth and we are your humble servants.

Tala did not speak she just stood there absorbing the information they had just given her. Aden could not understand what the elves were saying but could tell be Tala's reaction they had said something important. "What did they say Tala." "You mean you couldn't understand." "Of course not, I don't speak elvish." "Oh I see" said Tala. "He was speaking a different language this whole time?" she thought. "Well they, they said that I… I was a princess." "What? Do you know what that means? You are in charge you're the leader of the elves." The princess part was not what surprised Tala the most it was the fact that they knew who she used to be. They knew a name that she had forgotten soon after she came here. "What do you know about how I got here" she asked the elves. "Tell me how did I get here!" The elves remained silent then the head elf spoke "please that's all we know. You have to talk to the great mother for more. The elf pointed to the statue in the middle of the room. "I'm supposed to talk to that. It's just a lifeless hunk of wood. Please I need to know how to get home. This thing can't help me." Tala was about to kick the statue when she noticed that the statue had started blinking.

Slowly the statue started moving and changing. Wood turning into flesh and hair. Slowly the statue made the metamorphosis into a living being she had long red flowing hair and the distinctive greenish pale skin of an elf and was wearing a long dress that appeared to be made out of pure light. her face was the last thing to come alive in those moments time seemed to stop when her face was finally revealed Tala knew why it had looked so familiar to her why the carving outside had struck such a cord in her heart this woman that stood before her was undeniably Tala's mother.

The living statue hovered in the air for a few seconds then dropped to the ground with a great release of energy. All the elves in the room dropped instantly kneeling with their head bowed. "all hail Ælfwynn goddess of the elves." Tala gave them no attention "mom is that you" The woman quickly turned to Tala, her voice seemingly snapping the deity out of some trance. "Yes Tala I am your mother. I can't tell you how happy I am to see you. You've certainly grown up since I last saw you." "But you died when I was a baby, you can't be here." "I didn't die Tala, I simply decided to leave my earthly body, like you did that's why you're here. Beings like us leave earth when they feel in their hearts true longing for this world. I came back when I was needed and you have come here because you are needed as well."

"But mom, I don't…." "It's okay Tala I know, and I think it's about time you got some answers just hold on a moment." Ælfwynn turned to the head of the elfin platoon that had brought them there "raise" she said. In an instant all the elves were back on their feet. "As you wish my great Ælfwynn, what is your command whatever it is it shall be done?" "You have done well my child in bringing my daughter here, but now we require some time alone. Take your men and leave but stay close my daughter will need your assistance. I shall call you when we are done talking." "What about the other one" the elf asked pointing to Aden. "He can stay he needs to hear this too." The elf nodded "very well it shall be done" without another word he and his men left the room. When they were gone Ælfwynn started speaking.

"I'm sure you've got a lot of questions Tala, but I don't have much time in this form so we must make haste. I'm sure that by now you know the one known as Raven has been terrorizing this land for several years, and recently he gained control of a legion of angels They are supposed to be the servants of the gods and carry out our greatest acts on earth. I have no idea how he came by the means to control them but I'm sure you're well aware of the recent attack on Callack city. Now that Callack has fallen nothing stands in his way. He has started his final attack he plans on conquering all of Elysia and beyond. You cannot let that happen I need you two to stop him by any means necessary. My elves will help you I'll put them under your command Tala. "No offense goddess but I don't think that's gonna be enough" interrupted Aden. "I was there at Callack I've seen what those angels can do and were going to more than your army, fierce as they are. The sheer number and strength of the angels will overwhelm them." "Don't worry help will join you when you get there, but what I want the two of you to worry about is Raven and his dragon. They are very powerful you'll have your hands full dealing with them. The main reason I came was to tell you how to defeat him you have to." "STOP! It's to much" Tala yelled "I don't care about any of that, mom this is the first time I've seen you in so long I can't remember. I want to know what happened I want to know where you've been and why now that you've returned you're a god. None of this makes sense I'm tired of waiting. I want answers how did I get here, what's going on" Tala stopped her episode but stayed there staring at her mother shaking violently. "Tala I know you need answers and I want to tell you everything but I need to tell you this before…oh no" she stopped "I'm out of time Tala, just know I love you." The goddess's statue froze suddenly and returned do it's lifeless form. "No!" Tala screamed "come back" she ran over to the statue and began beating it in the chest "I have to know, I have to know why I'm here." Aden wrapped his arms around her and pulled her away from the statue she could have easily broken free, she had grown much stronger than any normal human but she found his embrace comforting and relented. "stop, if you need a reason I'll give you one you're here the same reason I am to do what's right remember like you told me. What's right is to stop Raven, and in time I'm sure we will find out who you are, we just have to beat him first. "How" Tala whispered though tears.

****

It had been almost two weeks since Aden and Tala had arrived in the elven village but they had quickly fit into the life style the elves lived. The simple life of being a druid, well that is what any man from the city would say. In truth the elves lives in the forest had a level of complexity that few could understand or even fathom. The elves communed with nature, helped it, made it stronger and in return the forest returned its gifts with the elves. The strength to tear a stone in two like a growing sapling, very long lives like the ancient trees around them, and the skill and speed to disappear in a moment. Like a clever fox that swooped out to take pray and then disappeared without a trace. Aden continued to marvel at their constant feats and ingenuity. He wished they could say the same about him.

Unlike Tala the elves didn't much care for Aden being in the village. They treated her like a queen because well she was one. Tala wore a permanent look of embarrassment wherever she walked, because the elves bowed before her and did not rise until she was long past them. Him on the other hand they treated as if he had the plague. At first he thought it was because he was human then he learned it was more than that. It was the nature of his magic fiery and destructive the elves could see it in him and shied away, as if his fiery touch would wilt them like a flower. He had taken to spending as much time with Tala as possible because the elves treated him much better when she was around. Also he found having Tala with him comforting. Her presence made him feel less lonely in the dark forest, but it was hard. The homes that they had been given to stay in were almost as far away from each other as possible. Surely a deliberate action of the elves and even though it was warm and he had a bed, Aden remembered the days they had slept only a few yards away from each other and longed for them. It made him sad but Aden had more important things to worry about.

 While they were there they had trained vigorously both physically and magically and during the time they weren't training they were busy conferring with war generals and officers finalizing attack plans and strategy Aden was currently at one of those meetings, seated what seemed like a mile away was Tala. She looked good it had been a while since he had gotten a chance to see her. The village's most powerful shaman had taken over Tala's training and she was progressing in leaps and bounds. She could control her magic much better she was more able to summon Familiars like the vine creatures that had attacked them in the forest, but she still could not reproduce the golem she had summoned the first time they had met. The most amazing thing was her ability to create any plant life she wanted, and grow it to maturity in seconds. Tala could grow a garden in a minute and a grove of trees in a few more. In enough time she could grow a whole forest. The elves marveled at this power, because even they did not have it, and assumed it was a gift from Tala's mother. Aden had been given a small section of decaying woods to practice in, and his skill increased steadily. He was worried because he hadn't been able to summon brand. The village shamans said the wards on the village may be preventing the magic and he shouldn't worry, but still Aden was afraid he had never spent this much time away from brand.

They were currently strategizing the arrangement of several phalanxes of soldiers for the upcoming battle. They were trying to figure out who would lead the advance troops from the front of the army. They were discussing archers when Aden spoke up "we've received word from the Vel villages and their forces are going to meet us outside of Vel." Ravens forces had been seen marching for Vel, the last stronghold of humanity in Elysia. When the elves broke their hundred years of silence and offered to help the Vel battle this new threat, they had gladly accepted. "Now the Vel use spears their skills are best put to use at the front of the army. They may not be as hearty as elves, but they know what happened in Callack and they're not going to go down without a fight. Now we know that Raven is bringing shadow people this time not just angels. They have some magic but its weak and they are human so I and a couple of elf volunteers could lead the Vel in battle against the shadow people, and that will let Tala and the other forces concentrate on the angels. If I know Raven he won't fight himself until all of his army is defeated and once it is we will take him down."

The elves listened although they didn't trust Aden he was considered an expert on humans and if there was one thing humans knew it was war. Aden especially proved a genius at war strategy. Tala was proud of him and admired his intellect more and more every day. She had been hurt at first when he had told her of his original intention to use her to get in the forest, but she forgave him almost instantly. Her story was pretty unbelievable after all. What really troubled her now was the reappearance of her mother and the suddenness of her departure. She still had so many things she wanted to know, but for now the important thing was that they stop Raven and get Bella back safe wherever she was and that they needed to do together. Although unfortunately, she thought, she and Aden hadn't seen much of each other lately.

"I agree with Aden she said finally "he paints a picture."
"Then it's settled" said Shorn head of the elven guard. "We
leave as soon as were ready." They were only days away from
marching to attack on Ravens forces. The previous dawn they
had received word that Raven marched from the dark city to
conquer the final obstacle between him and total domination of
the humans. He was a week's march from the Vel villages the
elves had already contacted the Vel on Tala's behalf to make a
united assault against Raven. In truth it did not look good.
Raven's forces outnumbered them 4 to 1. Not even considering
that the angels were fierce and powerful warriors stronger than
any man. Tala was not entirely sure they could win but Aden
gave her hope. The meeting was concluded and everyone went
back to their preparations.

Tala had a final lesson with her teacher before they
marched off to war. She was tired from all the recent activity so
she rode Woodrush the deer to the training grounds. Her teacher
had told her to meet him there, she arrived at the training
grounds, a lush green clearing surrounded by large trees and
infused with magic from countless years of magical training.
The place helped focus magic and was ideal for honing magical
skills. It was as if just by practicing here the thousands of
wizards from the past had cast a spell to help others learn. She
dropped down off Woodrush and gave him a specially made
treat prepared by the elves, as payment for the ride. Woodrush
was no horse and did not give rides for free .Tala found the old
wizard meditating in the middle of the clearing and did not say
anything but instead joined him sitting across from him in the
middle of the clearing.

Tala knew by now that her teacher did not rush anything
and sometimes waited for hours before deciding the time was
right to begin the lesson. Tala had noticed it seemed to take
longer if you tried to hurry him, so she just waited patiently.

The elf was old he did not have any wrinkles for elves never got any but they did age. His hair had gone white and he had a long beard with equally long hair in the back. Elves did not shave because it was often the only way to tell their age. They had long lives and facial hair was a symbol of age and rank. Elves that are banished or commit crimes are shaved to mark their treachery a lasting sign, as elves grow facial hair late in life and it took ages to grow. If elves were anything they were patient, especially her teacher.

He was so old there was no longer anybody alive that knew his name. He was only known as the master. When people asked what his real name was he claimed not to remember, though Tala wasn't sure as it seemed to be one big joke to him. Even without wrinkles his age showed. He had thinned out looking like a living skeleton and his skin had gone from the typical light greenish hue to almost transparent. He was not weak in his old age in fact he might have been the most powerful elf in the village. Pure magic flowed through his veins and had extended his already long life even longer. He had not gained this power though his will or some spell but from sheer knowledge and understanding of magic and how it works. It flowed into him, sensing him as one with the natural flow of magic. He had often said he did not like his prolonged life but accepted his place as a servant of Ælfwynn and a junction in the flow of magic. Another unique ability Tala had gained was that she could almost see magical energy. It looked something like what people would describe as an aura and the old wizard's aura was like a sun with a corona that was in constant motion.

Her master interrupted Tala's thoughts "you have progressed well" he said "you meditate perfectly you are one with your magic even lost in thought. Before you could only find it in your sleep, or when you were in danger, but to truly grasp the power of magic and reach the next level you will have to identify the magic in others and be one with it. Your opponent has reached that level and in order to beat him you will have to learn these methods, but do not worry too much about it. These things can't be rushed." "But master, what if I can't do it in time." "Then it is not meant to be. You have to trust in your power it may not always do what you want, but it knows what is best for you and it will always be there for you when you need it." "You talk as if it's a living thing, I thought magic was just a type of energy that certain people can channel and then direct in certain ways based on their individual powers." "Well yes that is all true and no it is not. Magic is a power unlike any other there is, much, much more to it then spells and summonings. These things are just the surface of an ocean so deep you could never swim to the bottom. Underneath that superficial layer is a whole world were magic is not separated by type and strength. I do not cast spells or even use magic, magic uses me. I do what it wills me to that is the true secret to being a master wizard."

"Master why don't you come with us with your power we could easily defeat Raven." "Ah, Tala I think you already know the answer to what you are asking. This battle is not my destiny it is yours my place is to train you." "Okay" Tala relented pretending to understand. "What is the lesson today?" "I'm sorry Tala there is none I've taught you all you are ready to learn. There is more, but you'll have to find it out for yourself, instead I offer you congratulations Tala you are the most powerful wizard in the village stronger even then your friend Aden. You have finished my training but there is a reason I called you here. I can't join you in the battle but I can lend you my power in another way." "What do you mean master." "Here, come take my hands we will have to sync our powers. Concentrate on your own power until you can feel the physical connection to mine it has always been there, but by bringing it to light I can give you my power. It will be the hardest thing you've had to do but I think it will work. Okay now concentrate Tala."

Tala took her masters hands and looked deep inside herself to her magical center the large ball of energy that exists within each person that wizards can tap into for performing spells. She drew from deeper into her power then she ever had before her mind burned from the pressure as she drifted toward the center looking for the connection to her master the pain was almost unbearable. Power raced through her. It filled every inch of her body the intensity burning her. Just when she thought she might burst her mind reached the deepest part of the magical power. Instantly the pain stopped altogether and she found it, the connection. A tiny invisible string that linked her to her teacher. She grabbed it and physically recoiled she had not been prepared for his power it was enormous.

Her power seemed a small pond next to an enormous ocean and like a pond her power was stagnant unmoving where as his moved in an endless tide. Power was coming in and out like countless rivers and tributaries and at the center of that power her teacher's consciousness waited. He was still and calm if she did not know any better she would think he was asleep. When she had a good sense of the connection between them she reached out for his consciousness. She reached further and further, she was just about to touch it and then, there was an explosion of energy just as she touched his consciousness. A mighty river of power flowed down the connection and into Tala she screamed inside her mind and probably in real life. The burn she had felt from her own magic seemed a candle compared to the eruption of power that now flowed into her she felt as if she might explode. Her own center of power did not grow the power just condensed inward getting denser and denser, hotter and hotter. Through the pain she saw that even with so much power flowing into her, her master's power did not get weaker, but it did seem to change. Then all at once the pain stopped like before as her magic seemed to cave in on itself and explode outward. She was forced out of her mind and back to consciousness.

She awoke to find the grove was very different then she had left it. She had been knocked back almost twelve feet from where she had been sitting. Slowly she sat up and examined herself. Steam was rising from her body, signs of the strength of the pure magic that had just flowed through her. All her clothes had been burned off she would have been naked if she hadn't been in armor. She also noted that strangely she could have sworn she had grown a few inches. Looking internally she found she could no longer enter her magic though her mind, the pressure immediately forced her out, but she found it easily accessible from the surface.

She turned to the clearing or rather former clearing. In an instant all of the living things in the area had grown out of control. The grass was three feet tall, bushes had grown 10 times in size, and a few new trees had also sprung up. She withdrew when a foot long ant ran by her hand. The whole clearing was overgrown by the transfer of magic except for a small area with an oddly colored scorch mark on the ground. This she realized had been where she was sitting. Tala quickly realized that was not all that had changed. In the center of the clearing was the largest, most perfect tree she had ever seen exactly where her teacher had been sitting. From it radiated the unmistakable aura of her former master.

"What have I done" Tala whispered to herself. "You have done nothing" a voice rang in her head. "The magic did" it was clearly her master speaking. "But master", "hold on Tala. I can't hold on to my consciousness much longer. I have to say some things you must know. It was my time, no one can live forever. I choose to use the last of my power to help you. I know I was supposed to help you that was my destiny that is why I lived so long and I am at peace with it. You should know the power I gave you has strings attached once you use it it is gone so save it for when it counts. If I have taught you anything in the past two weeks it is patience and that is the greatest lesson I can teach you. Now go Tala, go and figure out what your destiny is and don't let anybody tell you. You have to figure it out for yourself. That is after all, half the fun."

The voice faded away as calmly as it had come and Tala knew her teacher was gone forever. Tala did not know her teacher for long but the same could be said about Aden and look how she felt about him. She felt a connection with him she hadn't felt with anyone back home. She thought about Aden for a moment, when she did she realized them. All the strings like the one between her and her master but much stronger and much more numerous. There were billions of them connections between her and every living thing on the planet. Every blade of grass, every bug, every man, woman, and child interconnected in a giant web of magic. It seemed with her master's power she had also inherited some of his ability to commune with the magic of the world, but almost all these connections where weak. If she had tried to connect with any of them the creature on the other side would have died from the trauma, but one of the connections was different stronger, she grabbed it. The cord of power glowed red and grew stronger as its owner approached.

Aden felt the magical disturbance from all the way across the village as strong as a punch in the face. It had come from Tala that's all he knew, but it was enough. He immediately turned away from the archers he was organizing and unleashed one of his most powerful spells in a blaze of fire he streaked away at inhuman speed leaving a trail of fire and smoking footprints behind him

As he approached the grove where Tala trained he knew something was wrong. It looked nothing like it had before. The trees were too tall and he could not see into the clearing because a solid wall of green enclosed it. He did not look to inspect it and instead burst through the giant wall of shrubbery and surveyed the scene. Tala was standing in the middle of the clearing next to what had to be the largest tree in the world. She looked at him when he entered the grove she appeared to be okay but was definitely different. She wore no clothes except the magical under armor the elves had insisted she wear at all times she had an altogether wild look about her she looked taller than she had before and her already long hair was almost twice the length. It was like she had aged 2 years in one minute but the most significant change was her eyes. Her eyes told of deep unknown powers lurking behind them. When she looked at him he felt as though he was being looked at by a wise old elder. Her childish naive look had been replaced by one of regality and grace.

After a short period of silence Aden took as he shockingly took in the scene. He finally spoke "are you okay I felt the spell from all the way on the other side of camp. I came her as fast as I could I feared the worst." "Yes, I'm okay just I was finishing my training." Tala looked troubled but Aden decided to let it go for the moment.

"Where's everyone else I thought others would be here everyone for miles must have felt that, that, well whatever happened here." "You felt it because of our connection Aden, it's stronger than others, but don't worry it's over now my master and I are..." Tala trailed off. "Are you alright Tala" she didn't look good. "Well now that you mention it I am kind of tired." Tala started to faint Aden made a run to grab her but Woodrush beat him to it. He ran out of nowhere then stopped perfectly so Tala fell gently onto his back. The deer looked back at Tala to make sure she was okay then turned and give Aden a worried look. "I know Woodrush I'll help her come on let's take her to the healer." It appeared that Tala was right. No one else had noticed the disturbance when they arrived at the head healer Soran's house she looked as if she too might faint "dear Ælfwynn what happened to her." "She passed out after a training session I don't know what happened. I got there late and her master was nowhere to be seen. "Ok, I'll take her inside and see what I can do. However you go Shorn needs to be notified of this at once" "I'll just send brand and …never mind I'll go tell him." and with that Aden ran for Shorn who was sure to be organizing warriors at the officers command center.

     With her strong steady arms Soran lifted Tala off of Woodrush's back and took Tala into the large medicinal wing that had been constructed onto the side of her house. She laid her out onto one of the private cots. Tala appeared to be physically okay although she had definitely been though some sort of ordeal. If the cause was magical there could be a million ways in which she was seriously injured without there being any external signs of trouble. Soran cast a simple spell for detecting magical disturbances in the body, she spread her hands out over Tala's unconscious body a soft blue light radiated from them and enveloped her. The spell seemed to be working but as soon as it began to penetrate further into Tala's body the light flashed filling the room with blue luminescence. It forced Soran to avert her eyes she cut off the power to her spell and the light slowly faded away. Soran was afraid to try any more spells because it might cause an even more powerful backlash that could injure both her and Tala, so she checked Tala over healed some minor wounds and waited for her to wake up hopefully it wouldn't take long.

****

"The guards haven't checked on us in a while Issac. What do you thinks going on" Said Bella. "Something big is going on, Raven must have mobilized his troops to conquer more of Elysia. Bella this could be our chance." "But how do we get out" your necklace I think I've seen it before and if it's what I think it is it could be just the magical artifact we need, where did you get it" . "What this I just um... you know I found it. It was in a strange temple." "Please let me take a look at it." Issac began to reach for Bella's pendant. She withdrew clutching the pendant "I'm not sure." "Don't worry I'll give it back I just want to…" Issac stopped and pulled his hand back from the pendant a shocked look on his face. All of a sudden the pendant grew hot beneath Bella's fingertips. She looked down the pendant was glowing intensely she let go of the pendant and jumped back, The crescent shaped gem remained where it was stuck hovering in space glowing intensely. They both stared as Bella was slowly enveloped by the strange light. "Oh no" said Issac "you're not a werewolf are you"

****

Aden found Shorn giving one of his many lectures to the elvish troops. The patience of elves was legendary, but they were visibly showing disinterest. Aden immediately went up to Shorn and informed him of the situation. After Shorn heard Aden's story he was distressed to say the least. He ordered a party to go investigate what happened to Tala's teacher. Then followed Aden back to Soran's house, when they arrived they found Tala lying on a cot in the healing wing. Soran was standing next to her watching over her dutifully. Aden was the first to her side "how is she." "She doesn't seem to be physically hurt. However the cause of her troubles seems magical which means anything could be wrong." "Isn't there anything you can do?" "I'm sorry the best thing to do is wait"

"This isn't good" said Shorn with a particularly grim look on his face. "She is so important. When the goddess did not appear to us for so long we had almost given up hope. Then she came and gave us Tala, the elves may not realize it yet but the village needs her. Not to mention there is no way the elves will go to war without her leading the way. If she doesn't wake up soon her cause may be lost" Aden didn't say anything else he just kneeled next to Tala and held her hand.

It took three days for Tala to wake up when Aden heard the news he ran straight for Soran's house. He wasn't on fire this time but he ran so fast you might have thought he was. When he got to Soran's house Shorn was already there and Tala was already up and trying to leave. Soran was doing her best to prevent this "please your grace I beg you, you must rest after such an ordeal." "I just got done resting really I'm fine!" "Lady please." "No we have work to do, you tell my I've been asleep for three days then expect me to rest. Shorn!" "Yes lady" Shorn responded. Get everyone ready we march at dawn tomorrow." "But" Shorn began to interject then Tala shot him a look and he dropped it immediately. "As you wish it will be done." Shorn walked away quickly barking orders to every elf he passed on the way. When he was gone Tala turned to Aden just in time to receive the great hug he gave her. "Oh I was so worried I'm glad you are okay. You are okay right." Aden released her from his iron grip but held her by the shoulders as he looked into her face. "I'm fine Aden please don't make such a fuss" Tala was blushing intensely.

"Me make a fuss you seem to be making quite the fuss yourself. I remember someone telling me to calm down after I awoke from a several days sleep." "Maybe you are right, what happened while I was asleep." "You first, what happened to you, what was that explosion and where is your teacher, he has been missing ever since you passed out. Shorn sent out search parties but so far they've come up empty handed everyone in the village has been very worried about you both" Tala suddenly looked distant her mind was elsewhere. "I'm not exactly sure what happened it was the most powerful thing I've ever felt. It all happened in an instant, and then it was over, my teacher well he's gone." "I'm sorry I know how much you respected him, he was not so very different from master kroft." "Yeah he was a great man, but I'll have time to mourn him later. Right now we have something that we have to do. It is what he wanted me to do." "I don't know Tala are you sure we are ready I mean you just came out of a coma" "Were you ready when you came out of yours. I'm more than sure we've already fallen behind because of this. I'm fine trust me, I feel like I could move mountains and I probably could, if you dared me " she gave Aden a big smile "Well looks like somebody's awfully sure of themselves. Fine you are probably right, if we don't leave right away we won't beat Raven to the Vel. Could you do me a favor though, just let me take care of the final preparations for you. If you want something to do take care of Woodrush he's refused to eat since you passed out." "Okay fine" Tala relented. She got up eager to do something

Tala got up early before dawn the next day. She hadn't been able to sleep at all during the night, she felt like an overcharged battery. She went straight to Woodrush's pen she knew she should be making preparations but she had agreed to leave it to Aden. At least that is what she told herself, in truth she was terrified of what was to come. All of the previous day's determination had been replaced by dread. What had made her think she could do this. She thought back to how easily she had been outmatched by just a few angels and how defenseless she had been against the dragon. Sure she had gotten stronger but was it really enough. It was just weeks ago that she would have had a hard time beating another ordinary 16 year old girl in a fight. It was not just facing Raven and his army that scared her it was the enormous responsibility of the situation. Overnight she had become a leader of thousands. The entire village looked to her for guidance and all the hopes for defeating Raven laid square on her shoulders.

Tala sat there in the stall thinking of all this and brushing Woodrush's fur, even though it was magically perfect and never needed brushing. "What do I do woody, how do I lead an army. A few weeks ago I was just another kid at highschool. How did I get here it all happened so fast. Woodrush just turned to her and gave her a blank look as if to say "don't ask me." "Oh woody, were you worried about me, it's alright I'm fine." a pouty look came to his face. "Aww, you just keep looking so cute and we'll be okay." "I better get going." She stopped brushing him and gave him a kiss on the nose. Then she put they brush away. She stood up to leave but found herself having trouble finding the courage to exit the pen. She just kept thinking about the people waiting for her, just as she was about to force herself to leave Aden walked in.

"Aden good morning, how did you find me ?" "It was the only place I hadn't looked I couldn't sleep last night. I've been looking for you for you for over an hour." "I couldn't sleep either are you nervous about facing Raven." "Well yes of course but really I was more worried about you Tala." "you were worried about me really" she looked at him. Aden looked away shyly "and...and everybody else I don't want any of you to get hurt by Raven and his army because I failed to stop him." "Tala took his head so he was looking into her eyes. "Listen to me, whatever happens its not just your fight whatever Raven does it's not your fault it never was. You need to take this weight off your shoulders or you'll go crazy trust me I know." "You do know don't you. All the villagers are counting on you.

It can't be easy can it but it's a burden you can't avoid .Just like I can't avoid that Raven and I's destinies are connected. I'll tell you what let's make a deal. We'll share each other's burdens we will defeat Raven together and save everyone together, no matter what now what do you say."

Just like that Tala's fears melted away, so she wasn't alone Aden was with her and he had been all along. Whatever else happened along the road he would be with her. He may not have joined her journey for the best of reasons but she knew he was a good and noble man he would not let her down. "Aden…" "Yes Tala." "Is it true that elves really hate humans so much?" "I would like to think you ease their feelings on the subject a bit, but honestly their lifelong prejudice against humans is not something that is easy to get over. I do not believe in their hearts they really support defending the vel." "If you have shown me anything it is that you cannot go into something like this with something like that on their minds, get the warriors lined up I've got something I have to say."

Aden had done a good job organizing the troops into their phalanxes and lining them up in the center of the village. A stage and podium had even been hastily constructed in the middle for Tala to stand on. She slowly walked across the stage and stopped at the podium. She looked out over the crowd the whole village was there to see the army off and hear what Tala had to say. This didn't make the crowd much larger than it was with just warriors. Joining the army was voluntary but all elves were warriors at heart the only ones not fighting were those physically unable to do so and they would come anyway if they didn't think they would slow down the rest of their brethren. The elves were strong but strength wasn't there problem indifference was. This wasn't their cause it was their god's. They cared little for the lives humans they only cared about the forest, a single blade of grass was worth more to them than a dozen humans. That wasn't right Tala needed to relay the importance of the war to her recently discovered brothers and sisters. She wasn't sure before what to say to them, but the events of this morning had shown her exactly what to say.

Without hesitation she began "thank you all for coming here today to listen to what I have to say. I know I haven't been here for long and for those of my elven brothers who don't know I have not always been an elf I used to be human, I'm not even from this world. So there's no surprise why many of you, whether you admit it or not don't want to go to battle. I know most of you only go in the name of honor, to repay the debt for how good my mother has been to your kind. I know you would like nothing better than to let the Vel fall and return to your duty off protecting the forest. However you still remain loyal to your goddess and do whatever she asks. I think to go to war, to win a war you need more than just loyalty guiding your actions. You need to believe in what you're fighting for my mother told us to go to war because she knew it was the right thing to do and even though I barely know this world, standing here before you today I know it is the right thing to do. I can understand why you don't trust humans they are a faulty race violent greedy and destructive but by focusing on these aspects of humanity you have let these qualities seep into yourselves and the way you treat them.

The elves duty is not just to protect the forest but all living things and somewhere along the way we forgot our duty over our distaste for humans, but I find there is in humans as in all things good as well as evil. Even though it may seem impossible, the good can triumph over the evil however all that is required for the evil to succeed is for the good to do nothing when challenged. Now there is a challenge on the horizon and you've got to ask yourselves if you'll rise to meet it. Raven is evil he seeks to destroy everything if he manages to defeat the

Vel there will be nothing to stop him he will ride across this land like a wave destroying everything in his path and when he is finished he'll come here to get you. So forget what my mother said I will not order you to fight if you do not want to. I'll let you decide will we join are brothers the Vel in battle or do we sit here and wait for Raven to come get us, so what do you say."

There was a long pause no elf made a single noise, it was dead silence. Tala began to get worried then a single youth an elf no older than her rose onto a large rock. Everyone turned and look at the boy he hesitated for a moment then said "I would like to speak. I have always been faithful to Ælfwynn, however I questioned the goddesses wisdom in choosing someone so inexperienced and unknown to us as our leader. I questioned it further when you tasked us with going to war on the humans behalf, but just now you have given me sight when I had none. The hatred I saw in humans blinded me from seeing the irony that, that hatred caused my hatred for them. I want to thank you for showing me that. You have also shown me that you have wisdom beyond mine and more than enough to lead us. No matter what any others say you will have me in battle." Another elf rose this time an old and grizzled warrior and he spoke "and you shall have me as well." Another rose this one a mother she had met "I shall fight for you." Soon everyone was joining in a chorus of battle ready warriors. Everyone turned to Tala, she was caught dumbstruck she could not have hoped for this reaction. Luckily Aden came to her rescue he jumped on stage and shoving a fist in the air yelled "we march now." "We march now!" the cry was echoed by thousands of voices Tala's included.

****

They arrived and meet the Vel army in the early evening two days later. They had amassed just outside the province. Ravens approaching army was visible on the horizon with the sun sinking behind them. They were only visible at this distance because the force was huge it would be hours until they arrived. The Vel warriors where organized into their predetermined battle positions. Tala took her place at the head of the army next to Aden and Shorn. Aden leaned over and pointed out a group of people approaching them. "Thats the king of the united Vel province Andor Carr and his honor guard" The king was a tall dark man he was dressed in what looked like a mix between Arabian robes and a dashiki but only the best of both types of fashion. He looked completely pristine and he had a black goatee that came down to a point that mixed with the look on his face reminded her like Aden had of a character straight from the movie Aladdin this time Jafar. Although the smile on his face was more mischievous than evil, at least she hoped so. There was boy walking next to the king if the king was Jafar this boy was Aladdin. He was about 14 wore a turban and long baggy pants and a vest with nothing underneath showing off his muscular form. He differed from Aladdin in that instead of joyful glee there was a look of deep sadness on his face."

"Aden who is that boy next to the king." "Oh, that's the king's son Seth Carr. I spent some time with him when I was here looking for Raven. I taught him some spells but most of it didn't take he is a skilled warrior but only a half blood." "A what", "half-blood wizards can use magic but very little because they have no magic center like you or I they are connected to the magical realm by some other means. Beings like werewolves, or those born during a solstice there are several kinds. Seth's power comes from his royal blood all royalty here in Elysia are half-bloods if not full blown wizards, Though the Vel have not had a wizard king for a few hundred years." "Hmm" Tala thought "so Bella can do magic too I wonder why she never said anything." Thinking of Bella immediately made Tala sad. What had happened to her? Her mind was elsewhere as she approached the king and prince.

"hello princess I don't believe we've had the pleasure to meet. I'm king of the Vel   Andor Carr and this is my son Seth. I'm glad I was able to meet you. I'd also like to thank you for your assistance in these trying times I could hardly believe it when your first runner arrived seeking an alliance." "well in times like these it is important to set aside our differences in order to work for the common good, all life is sacred to elves together we will defeat Raven and save many, It is good to meet you king and you too prince." The prince raised his head and put on a fake smile "Thank you very much princess you honor me it is good to meet you too." "I've been told you are familiar with my good friend, teacher, and adviser Aden..." "Yes, my son has taken quite a liking to Aden he helped my son expand on his rudimentary magic skills." Aden broke in "yes how are your magical skills coming along Seth." "Not very well, I never really did have much talent for that sort of thing even for a half blood." "Don't give up so easily Seth magic isn't just about power it can teach you much about life when this is all over ..."

"Anyway" Tala interrupted "this is Shorn he is in command of our forces. She gestured to Shorn "king I'll have you know Tala is not just princess she is the undisputed ruler of all of elfdom, greater even than any queen." "Shorn please I would have been fine just being called Tala, no need to make a fuss." "No, he is right" said Andor "Proper titles cannot be forgotten among us royalty. My deepest apologies your majesty. I meant no disrespect I will do my best to observe my manners. I am impressed with your loyalty commander, It is an honor to meet you too. Now that we have dispensed with the pleasantry's let's make the final preparations for battle the hour is near Raven's army is almost upon us and it looks like we will be fighting with the moon at our backs.

The Final Battle

The moon was high in the sky by the time Ravens army arrived to do battle. It was a full moon that night one perfect for battle. The two army's lined up the Vel soldiers were wearing shining brass wide brimmed hats, armor, and face masks they looked like live bronze statues the moonlight glistening of their armor. The elves wear dressed much differently their uniforms were made of all natural materials but they were just as strong. All the armor was made from special ironwood strong as steel. Their clothes were a mix of greens and browns and they wore nothing on their feet. The only unnatural thing they carried were their weapons and they were so excellently crafted they too seemed to have grown from the earth.

Raven's forces were impressive he had legions of soldiers all dressed in black from head to toe. They were supported by dozens of shining and pristine angels their glistening armor looking out of place in the dark army. How Raven had gained control of his angels remained a mystery. Not even the wisest elves had been able to figure it out and the Vel didn't know either. The army marched toward them. It appeared Aden had been right about Raven waiting to fight. He remained high above circling on his dragon. The king, Seth, Tala, Aden, Shorn, and Woodrush took their place at the front of the army surrounded by the king's guard. "Aden","yes Tala", "you never told me what Ravens powers are." "Unfortunately, Raven has the strongest powers any wizard can have. With his power he doesn't necessarily tap into any natural force or aspect of power. Raven is able to manipulate pure energy it is the strongest and most versatile of all magic. I don't know what to expect so expect everything." "Well then I guess we are as ready as ever." Tala leaned to tell Shorn to signal the army. "Wait a second there's just one more thing."

Aden picked up a twig off the ground he held it in his palm and stared at it for a moment and it burst into flame after the fire had burned out he squeezed the ashes in his hand and concentrated for a while nothing happened. Aden had almost given up hope when his hand started to glow. He smiled, but instead of the small flaming bird he was expecting a huge pillar of flame came down from the sky and enveloped his hand. Both army's eyes were on Aden. The enemy wizards started preparing spells to negate whatever magic he was planning to perform. The Vel and elves started to cheer hoping he was about to deal a great blow to the enemy.

The pillar just stayed there for a while like a great beacon. Then slowly a bird shape grew from the center until finally Brand was visible but he wasn't the same now he was huge. His blazing form took up the night sky he was easily as big as Raven's dragon probably bigger he hovered there slowly flapping his great wings. "Brand what happened your huge" *"The gods thought you could use some more help the tradeoff*

was I couldn't be summoned until the battle." "Well it is
certainly good to see you now." "Aden you got back Brand and
he's giant now, that's good right?" "Indeed milady, Aden have
him hold of Raven and his dragon while we fight the ground
forces." "Sounds good Shorn what do you think Brand." Brand
did not answer but instead let out a great cry and surged
forward. "Okay then let us follow his lead" Shorn gave the
signal to charge and the rest of the army followed Brand. Raven
raised his arm and the dragon let out a great stream of fire and
Ravens army advanced to meet the charge. The battle had
begun.

Brand was first into the fray he slammed straight into
Raven and the dragon. The collision produced a large flaming
shockwave. They cartwheeled though the air over the fighting
armies clawing, pecking, and biting. Flames and great gusts of
air blew down on those below. Without hesitation Tala entered
the battle sword drawn. She danced around the enemy cutting
them down left and right. Her new powers and training made it
seem like everyone else was moving in slow motion, and her
strength was unparreled. She sent a soldier flying seven yards
with a punch to the gut. She turned parrying a blow at the last
second, sending her attackers sword into the heart of the soldier
next to him. At the same time she performed a spell and sent a
wave of vines flowing from her hand to trip up a group of
warriors closing in to attack.

As fast as Tala's attack was the rest of them were right
there with her. Aden, the king, Seth, and Shorn where expert
swordsman the five cut though the enemy forces like butter.
Woodrush brought up the rear sending enemies flying with his
horns. Normally Aden was cool and calculating, his mind ruled
by logic, but on the battlefield he was a berserker; the cries of
his haunted past sang out with every swing of his blade, and the
only thing hotter than the flames he summoned was the fury

that burned inside him. Aden quickly dispatched the men Tala had tripped. His sword burst into flame as he continued on. He waved it over the head of the men to his right ant sent a wave of fire flowing from the blade onto the warriors. After that he quickly sent a fireball into the face of a man running from the left that turned into a flaming fist and blasted through him and the heart of the man behind him.

Shorn had enchanted his blade to start slaying of its own accord it bobbed merrily from opponent to opponent in a dance of death. Shorn stood in the middle of its circle of attack and threw enchanted leaves at the enemy that hit like throwing knives. Something wasn't right with this fight, he didn't like it the section of the army tasked with dealing with the angels was doing even better than they were. The angels were falling without even putting up a fight it should have taken them hours to put a dent in the enemy forces that large, and that was assuming the best of circumstances. He turned to Aden and they shared a look, he was beginning to think the same thing

.

****

"Issac do you think we will get there fast enough to make a difference?" "I'm not sure Bella we are pretty close but from what we overheard from the guards in shadow city, all of Ravens enemies will be gathered to do battle. If we are lucky it will be a pretty even fight and hopefully we'll tip the scales, as long as you can control your pets." "That's one thing you don't have to worry about Issac now let's go."

****

Tala stopped on a hill and looked over the battle. It had been going on for a couple of hours and there were almost no angels left on the battlefield. They were being completely slaughtered. The shadow soldiers had dug in and were holding the line but all together the battle was looking good Seth and a fraction of the royal guard had been cut off from Tala and Aden and were off fighting several hundred feet to the left and Shorn and king Andor had also been separated from them during the fray and were fighting off to the right. Tala and Aden had managed to pull ahead enough to get a break as the next wave of fighters was a ways off. Aden walked up to Tala "something is not right here." "What are you talking about we're doing great look almost all the angels are gone." "That's what I'm talking about, those angels took out the entire magic academy with hundreds of the world's best magicians in a day how are we beating them with such minimal loses. Look the shadow warriors should be much easier to beat then the angels and there holding the line. I Know Raven he's up to something I think we should...." Aden was cut off by a black fireball that whizzed past his head Tala and Aden jumped back and turned to their attacker's swords drawn.

The enemy wizards appeared to be related. It was a man and woman they were both dressed in matching black shadow garb and shared the same blonde hair and deep green eyes. The woman was the first to speak "Aden and the elf queen, lord Raven will be pleased when we destroy you." "If my brother wanted to beat me he shouldn't have sent such amateurs we are more than a match for you two." "No Aden I have just the spell for dealing with you and your elf friend behold." The female wizard sat down legs crossed and began chanting softly as the male wizard created a dark bubble of energy that encased them both. "Get ready for anything Tala." "You don't think I know that I'm not the same girl you first met don't worry about me."

Tala and Aden stood side by side waiting to strike. The sister was still just sitting there chanting. The male continued to mold his protective bubble giving it writhing tentacles of dark energy like a jellyfish. They whipped and slashed at them leaving deep furrows in the ground. Aden and Tala jumped back and dodged the tentacle attacks waiting for the women to make her move. "The fact that the woman is taking so long to complete the spell could be a good sign. It could mean she's inexperienced and needs to repeat the incantation or...", "or what Aden", "or … whoa that was close." Aden jumped out of the way just in time to miss a giant tentacle slam into the ground right next to him. "Or it's a very powerful spell and takes a long time to perform"

Tala used her elven blade to cut through a magic tentacle "with our luck do you really think it's going be the good one Aden." "I guess it was just kind of hoping that..." Tala held up a hand. "Wait Aden listen" there was a low rumbling noise and the ground was starting to shake. "The rumbling", "that's not all look she stopped chanting." The rumbling increased and a small mound of dirt started to rise in between the two sorcerers. The girl had indeed stopped chanting and furthermore she appeared to be unconscious. The dirt mound continued to rise until it was over ten feet tall then it twisted into the shape of the man with four arms. "Tala it's a golem like the one you summoned don't underestimate him." When the golem finished forming it stepped free of its earthen prison and took a step forward it turned to face Aden and Tala and slowly lifted its heavy lids revealing eyes the same rusty color as the rest of its body, then the beast spoke in a low grumbling voice "Now *you see my true power whom is the amateur now*." "Tala I know how to handle this a little time in the kiln will fix this pot. Aden stepped forward and unleashed a fire spell on the artificial man "Flara" fire streamed from Aden's palms to envelop the man Aden keep a steady stream of fire on the creature, it showed no signs of retaliating to his attack after a few more seconds he let up. The creature was still there glowing red hot, when it cooled it had hardened into a solid terracotta statue "see Tala I told you", "aren't you the one who said not to underestimate it, look"

She was right the golem's arms were slowly moving, then it slammed its fists together and the top layer of its body shattered, revealing untouched dirt underneath. The golem spoke again in its heavy voice "*none of your magic will work on me I'm immune to your fire.*" "How about this then Aden pulled out his sword and stabbed at the golem but it was ready this time. The monster stomped hard on the ground it created a tremor that tripped up Aden and he stumbled forward his sword swept by the golem's waist. As he passed by it brought two of its fists down on Aden's back knocking him to the ground. The golem brought its foot down intent on crushing Aden's head but Aden quickly rolled out of the way. He jumped to his feet and attacked with his flaming sword spell he slashed down this time he managed to cut of the arms on the left side of the golem's body. It growled and gave Aden a great backhanded swing with its two remaining arms that sent him sprawling on the ground. The beast smashed the hardened stubs that had once held arms. "*You underestimate me, this is merely a scratch I told you your magic can't hurt me mine is stronger observe.*" The monster had a look on his face like a smile as his arms slowly grew back. "Yours is stronger... then it's as I thought" Aden retreated back to Tala.

"Tala I think I get how the spell works I can beat this thing, but I've got to get to those sorcerers. Tala I need you to hold the golem off can you do that." "Please Aden give me some credit, and admit you just can't beat him so you need me to do it, it's no problem I can do it." "You've got a lot of confidence for someone in their first battle." Tala smiled at him "of course you trained me well, now go do what you have to do I've got this thing." "OK good luck" Aden ran off and Tala squared off against the golem. "*You think you'll do any better than you friend bring it on, I'll get you just as I got the girl you were traveling with."* "Bella what do you know about her? Tell me now!" "You'll have to beat me first." "Not a problem."

Tala was a better match for the golem than Aden her new powers made her just as strong as the golem but also gave her incredible speed the monster couldn't hope to match. She weaved in and out stabbing and slashing and cutting off limbs but the golem grew them back as fast as she cut them off. The golem managed to trip her and this time it delivered the follow up stomp to its victim. Tala rolled over in agony the monster tried to stomp her again, but she dodged and got to her feet clutching her ribs with her free hand and her sword with the other. At least three of her ribs were broken the magic inside her was already beginning to heal the damage but it would be a while before she was back to normal. She needed to finish the fight,

It would be impossible to outmaneuver the golem like she had before. "What's the matter elf beaten already" the golem charged at her. Tala froze she didn't know what to do maybe she wasn't ready for this battle after all. As the golem charged ready to finish her off, all she could think was "is this how I die."

Aden was doing a good job dodging the energy tentacles. He had gotten close to the protective bubble the male wizard had set up but he hadn't yet figured out a way to get through the bubble or defeat the wizard inside. Aden ducked under a tentacle that would have taken off his head. What he needed to do was get rid of these tendrils. He couldn't think with them attacking him, but how. Every time he destroyed one more appeared. "What about a defensive spell" he thought "that could work" and he knew just the one. "Igniskild" Aden cloaked himself in a dome of flame. The spell had the desired effect the energy tentacles attacked his dome but were destroyed as soon as they touched the fire shield. He didn't want to use energy on another powerful spell but he had to act quickly before the male wizard reacted. "Velocido!" Aden mixed his fire step spell with his shield spell turning himself into a fiery battering ram he rocketed into the enemy's shield it shattered on contact bowling over the male wizard in the process.

In a moment the golem would be on top of Tala. It would all be over any second. just as the golem was about to destroy her, Tala pulled herself together and used the first spell that came to her mind and it wasn't one of her spells she used, she threw up her hands when the monster was an inch away from her she yelled "Flara!." Amazingly a jet of flame burst from her hands and baked the golem on the spot. Tala fell backward to the ground in front of the new statue. Its arms frozen outstretched to attack and a murderous look on its face. She groaned and clutched her wound the spell had taken too much from her in her wounded state. After a few more seconds of grumbling Tala managed to sit up. She held her hands in front of her and stared at them. How had she performed that spell, she had come to expect the unexpected, but everything she had been told about magic said it wasn't possible. She was a earth wizard she shouldn't be able to do fire wizard spells. In any case she didn't have time to think about that now. She had to see how Aden was doing.

Tala started to look around "crack!" a loud noise made Tala turn back to the golem. "Crack!" the noise sounded again and Tala saw the golem's arm move a little. This wasn't good the golem wasn't dead after all she just slowed it down. There was another series of small cracks accompanied by a low growl. Tala forced herself up she had to think fast she knew she could end this battle if only...that's it! She knew what to do. She just had to concentrate on the connection between the two of them and he was sure to come help her. Tala tried to concentrate but it was hard the golem's solid outer layer was cracking faster and faster and it was gaining more movement every second. Finally there was loud stomping and Woodrush bounded over Tala's head and crashed into the golem with its mighty antlers. He shattered the golem's hard outer shell on contact and sent it flying ten feet were it landed on its back and came to a skidding halt.

Shortly after it landed on the ground the monster burst into movement it shouted as it struggled to get to its feet. "I told your friend that none of his magic would work on me so what made you think that when you used the spell it would work. It is interesting to see an elvish fire wizard though but I'll say it again fire magic can't kill me." "Fine but I'm not a fire wizard and this isn't fire magic. Tala shoved her fists in the ground and funneled pure nature magic into the soil. The golem was the perfect position for her spell the golem tried to get up but it was too late. A small sapling that burst though the monsters chest. When it tried to grab the tree it found his arms and legs bound to the ground by vines. Slowly small trees plants and shrubbery grew from the center tree covering the dirt golem's body and anchoring it to the earth with their roots until the golem resembled a small humanoid shaped garden. The golem wasn't dead but the plants held it totally immobile.

"What have you done to me elf." "You see the bad thing about being a pile of living dirt is that you make great fertilizer." Then the golem started laughing, it made an evil cackle that made Tala's spine shiver. "Hah, ha, hah, ha, hah, you're pretty proud of yourself aren't you? You think you have me beat well your wrong. The golem started to glow and a ghostly woman slowly rose from the corpse of what was moments previously the living body of a golem now just a lifeless pile of dirt. It continued to rise out of the golem until she hovered eerily about three feet above it. The specter turned out to be the spitting image of the female wizard. "You see you may have destroyed the golem but when I get back to my body,

my brother and I will easily defeat you in your weakened state."
The spirit turned before Tala could respond and zoomed
towards where her body lay. When the wizard's spirit saw its
body it froze. There she saw Aden next to her defeated brothers
slowly dying body and standing over hers with his sword
pointed down at her throat. The spirit screamed "nooooo!" and
streaked towards Aden. Aden smiling at the woman said
"goodbye" then delivered the final blow. Instantly the spirit
dissolved and all Aden felt was a breeze as the last wisps of her
essence blew past him.

 Tala ran over to Aden her wounds had almost healed.
"Tala I must be tired I could have sworn I saw you doing fire
magic." "I don't know how but I think I did." "What?" The
only thing I can think of is that because the connection between
or magic is so strong that somehow I was able to use your's"
Aden just smiled and shook his head. "What?" "Nothing it's
just, you never cease to amaze me." "Tell me about it I'm with
you on that one. Anyway, whew! That was a close one. Aden
how did you know that she was the golem." "Well I thought it
was weird that a wizard so weak could have a familiar so
powerful and when the golem started speaking the things he
said made it clear it was the girl talking. Then, well once you
cut the body off a snake the head dies." "I think it's the other
way around Aden." "No, I definitely killed the body you were
right there" Tala sighed "that's not what I'm talking about, oh
never mind what are we...Bella!" "What about her", "the golem
knew something about her, which means the wizards knew
something" Tala ran over to the dying male wizard.
"What do you know about Bella?" The wizard managed a few
almost incoherent words in his last moments.
"We...took...never...find...her then the wizard coughed up
blood and closed his eyes, dead.

 Don't you die yet you bastard where is Bella!" "Wait,

Tala something's different listen it sounds like…" he stopped talking as he realized what was different. To their horror they watched, as all the Vel warriors stopped fighting the shadow army and had instead joined them in fighting the elves. Even without the angels the combined forces of the shadow and Vel armies were overpowering the elves. "What is going on Aden, why are the Vel attacking us?" Aden got a furious look on his face "I'll tell you what's going on Tala, treachery the kind that Raven specializes in."

"Don't take it personally Aden, Raven said he would not only spare our village but leave us our freedom if we killed you and his angels." Aden and Tala turned around to see king Andor standing behind them. "Andor you traitor do you really think he'll keep his word." "I had no choice Aden if we'd fought Raven we would have lost it was inevitable." The king was off ten yards or so surrounded by his honor guard. "You will pay scum!" Shorn yelled as he burst through a row of soldiers and attacked the king. He hurled several dozen of his dagger leaves all at once. The leaves embedded themselves with perfect accuracy within their targets and killing the entire royal guard in one move. However the king easily deflected all the blades directed at him. It appeared he wouldn't go down that easy. The king was a mighty warrior and one of the only half-bloods in history who could hold their own against a full blown wizard. Andor drew his sword, he and Shorn charged toward each other and clashed swords.

Seth was sick with himself this battle was wrong how could his father align himself with such evil. He knew his father was only trying to do what was best for the Vel, but Seth would rather die fighting evil then live and become it. He had finally agreed to go along with his father's plan for the good of the nation, but he could take it no longer. If the Vel lived through this battle how would they live with themselves? When the king had sprung his trap Seth realized his mistake and set about fixing it, he instructed his soldiers to continue to fight the shadow army and worked his way toward his father.

Aden and Tala fought back to back as the two armies attacked them from all sides they were completely cut off from the elves their only remaining ally. Not that they could have helped much, as Raven and Andor's forces were quickly overwhelming them. "I can't believe this, how could Andor do this to us." "Aden I think we have more important things to worry about right now like not dying." Brand and Raven's dragon continued to do battle overhead again and again they clashed in the sky sending fire sparking off in all directions their battle lit up the night sky. As battles continued all around Aden and Tala, a new presence approached the battlefield. Aden was the first to notice "Tala look who are those two people" at the edge of the battlefield two people stood atop a mound and they were not alone a legion of shadowy figures approached behind them. "I can't make the two of them out from here but ...oh no! Tala the rest they're, they're all werewolves." "Great that's all we need is a bunch of monsters to fight" "Wait I don't think they're with Raven I can't believe it look they are attacking his army"

It was true the werewolves had joined the battle but not on Ravens side. It appeared as though they had aligned themselves against the dark wizard. And they were doing quite well considering they were outnumbered ten to one. They tore into Ravens forces claw and tooth overwhelming sword and shield. "No time to ponder on our good luck Tala, we've got to get back to the battle."

Bella and Issac stood at the edge of the battlefield, watching over the fighting. Bella was dressed in black armor she had stolen on their way out of the shadow castle's dungeon and Issac had donned the golden armor of an angel they had defeated during their escape. Bella grabbed her pendant with one hand and pointed the other at the battle and shouted to her new allies "brothers and sisters the time is now attack!" a thousand giant hairy monsters surged forward, they entered the battle hungry for blood. "See Issac I knew I could get them to fight against Raven. I'm just glad we got here in time." "Well I guess you are right, but it doesn't appear we arrived in time to warn them about Andor's betrayal. So Bella what do you say we enter this battle, are you ready." "Oh I'm ready time to get back at this jerk, let's go."

Seeing the werewolves enter the battle gave Seth mixed feelings he was happy they had gained a new ally against Raven but upset that more of his people would die. He had to get to his father and do it now. Seth ran the last couple dozen yards cutting down any soldier that dared to cross his path. When he found his father he was still fighting Shorn. It appeared as though they were at a standstill, though the king appeared to be tiring. Blocking against a full blown wizard's spell was taking its toll on him. The king had easily deflected all of Shorn's magical projectiles. So Shorn had used a spell that had greatly increased his already superior speed and strength forcing the king to be very careful. If he even parried an attack the wrong way his arm could be broken. However he was still holding his own, then the king got lucky. Because he was a half-blood Shorn had underestimated him and let down his magical defenses. This gave Andor the opening he needed. All his spells used little magic but were quite effective, he sidestepped Shorn's next swing, raised his hand to Shorn and launched his spell.

"Shaterra" a stone materialized out of thin air and slammed into Shorn's head knocking him out, he collapsed to the ground. Andor stepped in to deliver the final blow but as he swung down Seth stepped in at the last moment and knocked his blade away. "Seth you dare to interfere", "father I cannot let this continue. I beg you to stop now. If we fight with Aden we can win this." "I knew I should not have let that delusional wizard train you, he has turned you against me. I love you son but if I have to for the good of Vel I will kill you." "I'm not doing this for Aden I'm doing this to save the soul of the Vel and to save all of Elysia. I would try to convince you but it seems your fear of Raven has blinded you. Like you I'll do what it takes if that means I have to kill my own father to save everyone else so be it."

Slowly father and son squared off. It was a fight neither of them wanted but would put their all into. Andor waited for Seth to attack, which he did in the form of a stab. Andor sidestepped, grabbed Seth's arm rolled him over his shoulder and slammed him to the ground. Seth rolled away to avoid the kings sword that bore down on top of him. Seth got to his feet just in time to block another attack from his father. Andor didn't let up he attacked again and again forcing Seth back. Seth was losing, his father was just more skilled but he had to win there was only one way, he wasn't any good at magic but he had to try. "Brace" he yelled, nothing happened the spell didn't work. "You know can't do magic while you're in battle Seth don't embarrass yourself." Andor swung again and Seth caught the sword with his own at the last second and sent his father's sword into the dirt. He tried the spell again he focused and thought, "What did Aden tell you, concentrate, draw upon the power around you and focus it into a spell using the power word, brace!"

This time a Shockwave came from Seth as the king thrust in his sword for an attack. His sword was bashed aside and Andor was thrown into the air. When he landed Seth was already there, with his sword to his father's neck. "It's over father command the troops to fight Raven or I'll be forced to finish you and do it myself." Andor thought quickly looking for a way out but there was none accepting his defeat he finally relented to his sons will."Okay son you are the victor. I have no choice, I only hope the Vel don't suffer too much because of your decision." "So do I father, so do I".

Aden and Tala seeing the fight from the distance arrived on the scene just in time to see Seth standing over the king. "You're just in time Aden, my father was just about to order the troops to help us take out Raven once and for all." "I am glad to see you came to your senses Seth. Raven is evil and never would have kept his word. King I'll have words with you later. For now just be glad that you were facing your son and not me. Now I believe we've got a war to get back to king if you would be so kind." The king used a spell to enhance his voice so he would be heard all over the battle field.

"soldiers of Vel this is your king Andor Carr there has been a development abort the plan we are backing the elves attack the shadow army." There was a long silence as everyone on the battlefield stopped fighting to absorb the new information. Then a great cheer went up among the Vel and they turned on the shadow warriors and fought twice as hard as they had before. The combined force of the elves, werewolves, and Vel quickly changed the tide of the war. They cut into the shadow army with renewed vigor in minutes all that was left of the enemy was fragments of the original force.

"Looks like you were right Seth it seems our people really would rather die fighting Raven, then compromise their principles. I thought I was doing what was best I only hope the Vel can forgive me." Seth removed the sword from his father's throat and helped him up. "Listen father..." Seth was interrupted by a fireball that whizzed by his head and crashed at Aden's feet. Only it wasn't a fireball it was Brand. He was back to his normal size, he couldn't move his body had been broken in the crash. "*Aden I'm sorry I wasn't strong enough.*" "It's ok brand you did great, now rest I'll take it from here" said Aden. Brand took one last breath then collapsed into ash. They all felt the air from the beating of the dragon's wings as it landed with Raven upon it, in front of them.

For the first time Tala heard Raven speak "what is the meaning of this Andor we had an agreement." "Not anymore Raven my son opened my eyes to your evil." " Is that so, well then allow me to thank him" Raven turned to Seth they locked eyes for a second before Raven sent a bolt of power headed straight for him. Seth barely had time to think before the bolt was upon him he froze. The next thing he knew the bolt hit his father square in the chest. He had stepped in front of it at the last second, sacrificing himself to save his son. His father took the brunt of the blast but the force still sent them both flying back several yards into a group of fighting soldiers.

Furious Aden confronted Raven "Raven after so long we finally meet I hope you've gotten stronger or else this is going to be a short fight" "oh Aden you have no idea" Raven jumped off the dragons back and landed a few yards away from Aden and Tala. Raven was dressed all in black, he wore form fitting light armor with small gauntlets and bracers. His pants closely resembled solid black army fatigues. He was very pale and skinny but very fit with and tight athletic muscular build and long spiky black hair with long bangs that came down to his eyes.

"Aden I don't suppose you would join me, so why don't we just settle our little fight right now. I knew you would be trouble that's why I sent the strix after you, but I guess if you want something done right you have to do it yourself. Now it's just you and me." "I'm here too we are gonna defeat you together." "Tala let me handle this","Aden we talked about this." "Now, now no need to fight you can both have a piece of me." Raven began to vibrate and shimmer like Tala was seeing double she shook her head, but he kept distorting. A glowing line started to shine down the middle of him and his body split along the line. Then two complete identical Ravens were formed. "If you didn't fight together the odds would be against you. Although I suppose they already are." "How did you do that without speaking the spell?" "Oh Aden always a scholar. Why don't you lay down the pen and parchment and enter the battle." "You want a fight fine. Tala you take the ugly one, I'll take the stupid one." "Name calling Aden a little immature don't you think?"

Aden's only response was the fireball he launched toward the chest of the Raven on the left but it never reached him. Again without saying a spell he raised a barrier of dark energy and the fireball slammed into the shield. The shield received no visible damage, Raven lowered it and launched a bolt of power back at Aden. Aden prepared to raise his shield but he didn't have to. Issac jumped in front of the bolt and yelled "indirecto" the spell changed the course of the bolt and it slammed into the ground a few feet from Issac's feet. He turned to Aden "Hey buddy nice to see you." "Issac! Boy am I glad to see you're still alive" "I'm not the only one." Bella stepped into view next to Tala "Bella I'm so glad you're ok, what happened to you." "Tala it's good to see you too. Raven had us locked in his dungeon but we escaped to come help you guys and get a little payback." "Bella watch out" but Tala was too late the other Raven had snuck up behind Bella. She felt a sharp pain and looked down to see a blade sticking through her chest.

Seth woke up in a haze the sound of battle all around him. There was something heavy on top of him. Seth came out of his haze as a werewolf jumped over him, but he still couldn't tell what was on top of him. Then he remembered what happened "oh no" he slipped out from under the motionless bulk of his father. Seth turned him over, he wasn't breathing. There was a large scorch mark on his chest were Raven had hit him. Seth felt for a pulse but inside he already knew there was none, his father was dead. Seth was deeply saddened but that sadness quickly turned into rage. "This, this was Ravens doing and he will pay."

Raven started to withdraw his sword from Bella's body when suddenly he met resistance a giant furry hand grabbed it midway. Where Bella had been there now stood a full grown werewolf. With a great roar the wolf broke the blade off at her chest spun around and delivered the broken sword into Ravens chest with so much force the creature's entire arm followed the sword though his chest. The creature roared with satisfaction and withdrew its arm as Ravens lifeless body slid to the ground. The werewolf turned to Tala she jumped back and raised her sword ready for anything, anything except hearing it speak.

"He wasn't so tough I don't know why everyone makes such a fuss over him" "Bella is that you." "Of course it's me Tala who else would it be." "It's just your transformed but your still you, you have control over yourself." Bella grabbed her pendant in one large furry hand and showed it to Tala. "Not just myself thanks to this pendant I can control my own transformation and the minds of any werewolf not wearing one." "Thats great Bella but don't get too ahead of yourself there is still one Raven left, what do you say we help Aden take him out." Bella and Tala turned and joined Aden and Issac.

"So" said Issac "It looks like we are all finally together." "we are, it is nice isn't it Aden", "you said it Tala but let's catch up later right now we have a battle to win." "very good, the werewolf surprised my clone but let's see how it does against a dragon" before the implications of Ravens words set in a giant clawed foot smashed into Bella and sent her flying through the air she crashed into a large group of shoulders with so much force the entire it killed four of them, Ravens dragon took off and landed next to where she landed. "My dragon isn't just any old familiar he is Raz a king in his own right and a creature of unequaled strength. Your friend doesn't stand a chance and so any of you don't try to help her." Raven started shimmering again and divided, but this time instead of two he divided into three clones. Issac, Aden, and Tala faced off against their Raven the feel was different this time everyone was serious, this time the fight wouldn't stop until a victor was decided.

Tala struck first she used all her strength and leaped the entire fifty feet between where she and her clone opponent stood. However he wasn't going to get caught by surprise twice Raven was ready with his sword drawn as Tala came hurtling towards him. At the last minute she spun, firmly planted her feet on the ground, somersaulted into the air and brought her sword down on Ravens head. He quickly brought his sword up to block her attack. Tala pushed down on Ravens sword launching herself into the air again landed behind the clone spun her sword around and stabbed at Ravens back, he raised his energy barrier to defend himself but Tala's magical sword cut straight through it. However raising the shield gave the clone enough time to jump out of the way and face Tala. He unleashed an energy bolt straight at Tala, she barely had time to channel magic into her hands. She used it to block the brunt of the attack but the force of the blast still blew her back several feet onto her back.

Issac's Raven clone opponent sent a flurry of magic bolts at Issac who used his spell to send them all off course and smashing into the ground before they reached him. Raven continued to put on the pressure launching shot after shot of magical energy at the librarian. Quickly the strain of holding off Ravens attacks was becoming too much for Issac. Rather than tire out he concentrated put more power into his spell and turned the bolts back on their caster, Raven had no chance to dodge as six blasts of energy struck him solidly in the torso. The force of the hit lifted the clone of the ground and slammed him on his back. Issac watched the clone for a couple of seconds but it remained still.

Issac approached the clone "did I do it, is he dead." Suddenly the Ravens body sprung to life and launched another bolt of power at Issac. Issac quickly used his spell to divert the bolt into the ground but he had let his guard down and paid the price. The bolt was only inches from his feet when he managed to send it into the ground. The force of the impact sent dozens of stones flying at Issac. They smashed into him with the force of grenade shrapnel. He fell to the ground badly injured bleeding and broken. Issac could only watch as the clone approached completely unharmed. He looked down on Issac and laughed menacingly "Did you really think my own spell would be able to hurt me, the greatest sorcerer in all of Elysia, no you are all mine.

Aden and his Raven clone where engaged in an epic battle. Aden launched fireball after fireball at the clone that in turn launched bolt after bolt back at Aden. Explosions sounded all around them as the missiles collided in midair. Then the clone concentrated his attack into a single beam Aden jumped out of the way as the blast ripped through the air where he had once stood. The attack was so powerful Aden could feel the energy crackling in the air even after it subsided. Aden launched a spell in kind "flara!" a concentrated stream of fire blasted out of Aden's hands straight towards Raven, who launched another beam of magical energy back at Aden.

The two attacks crashed in the middle with an enormous explosion but neither of them stopped they kept feeding power into their spells fighting for the upper hand Aden's fire burned so hot the stone on the ground beneath turned to liquid. The air around them was so full of ambient energy rock and other pieces of small debris started rising off the ground still they fed their spells. The beams moved back and forth as they put more into it. A fighting shadow soldier was knocked too close and was instantly vaporized. For what seemed like hours to Aden when in reality had been only minutes they struggled back and forth. Then the clone let out one of his sinister laughs "I think I'm done playing with you. Now I'll show you how powerful I really am." Suddenly Ravens beam tripled in strength and blew straight through Aden's fire. He jumped out of the way but his left arm was caught in the edge of the blast he fell to his knees and cradled his arm which was severely burned. "You burned me, but I can't be burned." "You can't be burned by fire what I hit you with was pure dark energy." "What happened to you I remember when your magic was just pure not pure evil." "Aden the thing about that which is purist, is that it is the easiest thing to corrupt."

Bella awoke on top of a pile of dead soldiers the dragon was watching her waiting. Her whole body ached, her werewolf form healed quickly but the dragon had dealt her a serious blow Bella slowly dragged herself off the ground and stared her attacker in the eye. She let her thoughts go unvocalized and embraced her animal side letting a long angry growl convey her feelings. Surprisingly the dragon did have something to say Bella was astounded when the giant monster spoke to her. "It has been so long since I've tasted lycan flesh. This is the most fun I've had in centuries." "You can talk", "as can you, this keeps getting better and better. You see I don't like killing mindless animals I am no mere predator. I AM RAZ king of the black dragons and devoted follower of the dark lord Democles. Remember this name because it will be the last you ever hear."

The dragon went to slam his giant clawed foot on top of Bella, but Bella was ready she leaped into the air just as the dragons foreleg slammed into the ground. She nimbly touched back down on top of Raz's foot and turned to face him. "Hello Raz I am Bella, let me ask what makes you think no one will tell me their name after I beat you." "You arrogant little pest your destruction is assured." Raz swung his other foot at her. She leaped out of the way and clawed her way up the dragon's leg on all fours. Raz roared in pain as the force of his swing broke his own foot. As he roared Bella ran across his shoulder leaped and kicked Raz hard square in the jaw. His roar was cut off as his jaw was knocked out of the socket. Bella flipped in midair landing on Raz's other shoulder and leaped toward the ground, but Raz anticipated her movements and caught her in midair. Bella struggled against his grip but he only squeezed tighter forcing the air out of her lungs she yowled as the dragon slowly crushed the life out of her Raz used his free arm and popped his jaw back into place.

"You fought well but escape is impossible, it's over werewolf "Raz opened his mouth and slowly dragged Bella toward his giant gaping maw. Bella struggled but it was as he said escape was impossible. His huge fangs were only feet from her now and kept getting closer and closer Bella could feel the heat of Raz's breath on her face. Then a flash of silver flew past her face and Raz let lose his biggest roar yet. Dropping Bella, he clutched at his eye, the hilt of a sword protruded from it. Bella hit the ground with a thud she groaned and struggled to get up but couldn't muster the strength. She fell back to the ground and coughed up blood. She had been hurt more than she thought Raz had broken some of her ribs, her bones were already knitting back together she would be able to stand soon, but probably not before Raz recovered and decided to finish her off.

In the corner of her eye she saw the shadow of a man step into sight. He bent down and offered her a hand up surprisingly he was able to haul her 600 pound bulky frame up with relative ease, and supported her as she leaned on him. Raz was still stomping and roaring as he tried to remove the sword from his eye. "Thanks for helping me who are you." "I'm Shorn and you must be Tala and Aden's friend Bella the werewolf. You and your kind have helped us a lot here today I am glad to help you." Just then Bella noticed Raz wasn't struggling anymore. On pure instinct she tackled Shorn out of the way just as a giant blast of fire hit the spot where they once stood.

They recovered quickly and dodged as Raz continued to attack. "Sennar" Shorn cast the spell that enchanted his sword to attack of its own accord it lifted off the ground from where Raz had thrown it after pulling it out of his eye and circled the dragon, cutting and slashing wherever an opening presented itself. Raz stood up on his hind legs and batted at the sword but it was too elusive. The sword was mostly ineffective against Raz's thick hide but it distracted him and gave Shorn and Bella the time they needed to recover and prepare for the fight with Raz. Raz's struggling became more frantic he shook with rage slashing and clawing at the sword and only succeeded in injuring himself further. Finally Raz had had enough, he stopped struggling inhaled deeply and exhaled an ocean of flame it poured over him and completely filled the space around the dragon blowing away everything around him. Including Shorn's sword which landed at the dragon's feet reduced to a pile of molten slag. Bella and Shorn watched as the flames receded to reveal Raz's red hot scales and cold murderous eyes. One thing was sure Raz wasn't playing with them anymore.

Tala rolled out of the way as the clone shot a bolt at her and shoved her hand into the ground. Using her nature magic she manipulated some seeds that where dormant in the earth she feed her power into the seeds growing full trees in seconds. They burst out of the ground in a line straight for Raven who managed to jump out of the way of the incoming stampede of foliage, but as he flew through the air a trunk burst from the ground and struck the clone on the side knocking him to the ground. Using her incredible strength she tore one of the trees from the ground and threw it at the clone. The full sized tree soared straight at the clone.

At the same time Aden's Raven adversary approached his wounded rival. Aden was badly hurt his arm had been burnt to the bone in many places and what skin was left was badly charred. He was in excruciating pain and couldn't concentrate enough to use any magic. The sword he held in his hand was mostly for show it took all his strength just to hold it up. "You won't win Raven it can't end like this." Raven easily knocked Aden's sword away and laughed. "Who's gonna stop me you, you can't even stand. As soon as my clones finish off your friends I'll destroy the rest of your army myself no one can stand up to my power!"

Suddenly there was a huge crash and wood chips rained down all over Aden and the clone "what ?" the clone was knocked back as the energy from the fallen twin rushed back into him. "My clone it's been destroyed" Raven looked mystified. "Looks like you are not so strong after all Raven." "Its death means nothing it has only made me stronger. I think we've talked enough time to finish this" Raven pointed a glowing hand at Aden but a voice stopped him before delivered the finishing blow "don't even think about it."

As soon as Tala let loose the tree a jolt surged though Aden's and her's link she fell to the ground grasping her head trying to shut out Aden's pain before it crippled her. She managed to regain her faculties just as the log was hitting its target, but it looks like the clone wasn't planning on going down easy. When the tree was inches from its target the clone self-destructed, wood chips flew in all directions. Tala was knocked out of sorts she stumbled around in a daze there was buzzing in her ears and her vision went blurry until Aden's pain raced through her and brought her out of it she looked around and rushed to Aden's aid.

So there they were Aden, Tala and Raven. Aden crumpled up in pain with Raven ready to finish him off and Tala sword drawn ready to end Ravens life. "Alright Raven just put your hands up and back away from Aden, slowly." "Or what you will kill me, like I care there are two of me left. There is only one of Aden, if both of us die it seems like plus to me." "We both know that's not true all the copies aren't equal are they, I see though your ruse. You are the original if they die no big deal but if you die it's all over." "Your ability to see the nature of magic has served you well I will give in to you demands however it will not change the outcome of the battle." Raven suddenly disappeared leaving a trail of black smoke and reappeared a little ways away. "everyone get comfortable because no one leaves until this is over."

Raven raised a ring of black flames ten feet tall to encircle the clearing Tala ran over to Aden and helped him up, he leaned on her for support. "This is it Tala the final battle, I know we promised to help each other but in the state I'm in I'd just be a burden." "Don't get so upset yet I can heal you not all the way but you'll be more than well enough to fight." She grabbed Aden's arm and used a very powerful healing spell that she had learned while in Ælfwynn. Aden screamed as his skin grew back the pain immediately intensifying dozens of times over. The pain was so intense it threatened his sanity. Finally the pain subsided leaving Aden exhausted but otherwise whole again. As it was the spell did not return his arm to perfect condition the entire thing was scar tissue and instead of the normal lighter than skin tone it was a brick red color. After she finished healing Aden Tala released his arm and stepped back.

Aden spent a moment inspecting his new scarred arm then turned to Tala and nodded. No more words were spoken it was clear what they had to do. They turned to Raven, the outcome of this battle would decide the entire war.

Seth headed in the direction where he had seen Raven when he first landed his heart was filled with revenge he ran as fast as he could what came into view was not the battle he had expected. Instead of one fight there were several Issac, Tala, and Aden were all fighting their own copy of Raven. Seth stopped and watched the fighting he didn't know what to do. Magic was a rare talent in the Vel province. So Seth was overwhelmed by the magic flying all around until Issac got blasted by a shower of rocks that left him defenseless. Seth looked around but the others continued their battles without taking notice. As the copy of Raven approached to finish off Issac with his sword Seth ran into action.

"You will pay for the pain you have caused Raven." "So Seth you survived, but why continue to challenge me you have no hope of defeating me Issac was much stronger than you are and look how he fared." Raven gestured to Issac on the ground who moaned and shook his head. "What chance do you have?" "Your words are poison they may have swayed my father but you will not dissuade me from my duty. I will kill you and I will do it with my own blade not magic." "Well you can try"

Raven and Seth swung their swords at each other with all their strength. Seth fought like he never fought before. He was like a whirlwind by the time he had made a strike he was already attacking somewhere else, but Raven was just as fast and he was keeping up with no problem. Raven pressed Seth attacking harder and harder putting Seth on the defensive. Then Raven caught Seth of guard he knocked Seth's sword to the side then slammed his fist into Seth's jaw before he could regain his guard. Stunned Seth blindly swung his blade at Raven but he duck under it and kicked Seth's legs out from under him knocking him to the ground. Raven jumped on top of Seth and pointed his sword at his neck "I told you Seth" with that Raven stabbed down

"Indirecto" the sword went off course into the dirt a single drop of Seth's blood was drawn as the blade buried itself in the ground directly next to his neck. Raven turned to Issac who was sitting up with his arm outstretched toward them "you will pay for interfering with me Issac" he roared but was cut off from saying anything else as Seth's blade shot out of his back. Seth got out from under Raven "that was for my dad may your death restore his honor." "My death ha! I am far from dead boy" Ravens voiced hung in the air as his body dissolved and a cloud of black dust flowed toward the last remaining Raven. "No!" Seth yelled "come back he chased after the cloud swinging at it wildly. About a hundred yards away from the other Raven a wall of black flame burst from the ground cutting him off from his pursuit and knocking Seth on his back.

The air inside the circle of black fire was tense there was no more holding back everyone was serious. "So this is finally it Raven one of as dies here. You better be as strong as you are boasting because I don't intend to die" said Aden. "See for yourself" Raven launched a series of dark magic bolts at Aden. "Tala we need cover" Aden yelled as he dodged the bolts .Tala shoved her arm deep into the earth she really needed to concentrate, and connect with the earth in order to cast this spell. Magic flowed through the earth and once again trees grew and burst from the ground however this time the scale was much greater the entire circle of flame filled with full grown cedars and pines creating a miniature forest. Tala slumped "Aden you are going to have to hold him for a while after that I need to regain my strength." "Sure thing Tala don't worry I can hold my own for a while." "I'm beginning to grow tired of your carefree attitude" Raven growled as he launched a ton of bolts all at once. Aden franticly looked for an escape but there was no hole in his attack "I will kill you and when I do Elysia will be mine." Raven clenched his hand into a fist and pointed at Aden, his dark bolts suddenly changed course and converged on Aden. The instant before the bolts hit him Aden leaped and released a quick powerful blast of fire from his hand launching him backwards out of the way just as the bolt collided in a massive explosion. Aden landed on his feet and recovered his fighting stance. "Raven don't think for a second that I'm not dedicating the entirety of my soul to destroying you. "Flara" Aden blasted fire into the sky and then it exploded radiating outward destroying the canopy around him. "That was quite a show but ultimately ineffective" said Raven. He reciprocated by launching a series of energy bolts at Aden. Aden launched a fireball at Raven as he dived for cover behind a group of trees, Raven also dodged the blast. Aden called to him from his hiding place "The fire blast was ineffective because it wasn't meant for you." "What" Raven barely had time to say the word before Tala launched her attack. Leaping across the flat treetops that Aden had just cleared with his fire spell. Tala dived at Raven delivering an extremely powerful dropkick. Raven just managed to dodge as her heel slammed into the ground leaving a small crater. Tala recovered quickly and attacked but by then Raven had erected a shield that stopped Tala's fist midstrike. She tried to pull her arm away but the shield held her fast. Raven laughed but his victory was cut short little did he know that Aden had snuck behind Raven during Tala's attack and now he unleashed the largest fireball he could muster straight at Ravens back. Raven had let his guard down for just a second but it was all Aden needed the fireball easily 10 feet in diameter struck Raven full in the back and hurled his body like a rag doll skirting across the ground end over end Raven landed in a crumpled heap 20 yards away.Aden approached Tala as the spell holding her faded. "It's over Tala he couldn't have survived that blast no mortal could" "That may be true but I'm not mortal not anymore."

They watched in horror as Ravens broken corpse stood impossibly up. It was facing away from them they watched as his legs snapped back into place just as he was standing. His neck and spine moved back into place with sickening cracks. His muscles knit themselves back together. The skin on his back that had been burned clean off regenerated but it didn't stop there. After he had completely healed he began to change dark feathery wings sprouted from his back and his skin turned black. When he turned around to face them he looked completely different his teeth had turned to fangs and his eyes were just catlike slits. What Tala and Aden saw now was not human it was a monster.

Raven's sinewy new form looked sickly and unnatural, but powerful "See Aden, see what you've driven me to. Now you see my true form, I never expected this battle to go this far but it ends now." "Aden what is he", "I don't know Tala but it's not Raven, not anymore, it's a monster and it needs to be put down." Aden shot a fireball at Raven who effortlessly caught and crushed the blast in his hand. "you cannot defeat me Aden you have limits I do not as long as I can channel my power I am invincible." "No one is invincible" Aden yelled. He had had enough this battle had taken a toll on him that he could not handle. This was it he was making his stand either Raven died right here right now or he did. Aden called upon the deepest parts of his power and crafted a mighty spell one that would not be rivaled this day. He channeled so much power the air around him ignited wreathing his body in flames and the power visibly leaked from him bathing the area in an orange aura. "Tala move away move away now!"

As soon as Tala was clear of the spell Aden let lose his spell in a giant explosion. thousands of fireballs materialized from nothing all around the battlefield and struck Raven like some awesome fireworks display. The attack continued raising the temperature until trees dozens of yards away ignited. Slowly the fireballs tapered off but Aden was not done yet. He channeled everything he had left into one mighty fireball it started small expanding from his core and it continued to expand until he was no longer visible at its center but still it continued to grow to over 30 feet in diameter. Then using his whole body Aden launched it. It flew like a comet with impossible speed at Raven devastating the landscape as it passed. It crashed into Raven and exploded emitting a blinding light that forced Tala to look away. She turned back and watched Aden slide to the ground utterly spent .The spot were Raven had stood was hidden behind a curtain of smoke and raining debris. Tala watched the scene open mouthed. To think that just weeks ago Aden's limit was one fireball barely 3 meters wide and now he was capable of this after battling for hours. Well look how far she had come she was not far behind him. She knew she could relax now, after that display it had to be over.

Aden had never been so drained in his life. He had put everything into that attack, he couldn't even find the energy to wiggle a toe. He looked up as the smoke cleared slowly. Surely Raven could not have survived that, no matter what kind of shield he raised or regenerative powers he possessed, right? "Then how come I don't feel like I won then" slowly the smoke reveled a shadowy silhouette of a man with wings "no it can't be." Unfortunately it was.

A huge energy bolt tore through the smoke and caught Aden square in the chest. He had no energy to dodge. Tala ran to his side and tried to heal him but he stopped her. "Tala" he

coughed up blood but continued weekly "don't…waste
power….it's up to you now….. stop him." Aden closed his eyes
and passed out Tala checked his pulse he was weak but alive.
Satisfied she positioned Aden carefully on the ground and
turned to Raven as he stepped from the smoke. "is that all
you've got!" he shouted spit flying from his mouth and his face
the perfect picture of madness. Tala slowly rose and turned to
Raven, her sorrow and anger building. She let out a primal
scream the ground rumbled and the earth began to shake
violently and the ground in front of her burst as her golem once
again rose from the ground.

     The animated monstrosity and Tala were linked and it
shared her rage. The creature rushed Raven caving in his chest
with one arm and bashing in his skull with the other. Raven's
neck snapped back and he struck back even as his ribs popped
back into place .With unnatural strength he punch straight
though the golem's chest but it wasn't quite mortal either and
easily continued its assault. Delivering a savage combination
and a vicious uppercut that knocked Raven skyward. He spun in
midair and blasted chunks out of the golem with magical bolts
but Tala was not out of the game. She used her magic to fill in
the gaps between the rock and earth of the golem's body with
wood but as the fight continued it became clear that it was a
losing battle.

     Despite his smaller size Ravens transformation had
granted him strength every way the equal of the 12 foot golem
and she couldn't keep patching him up forever where as Ravens
regenerative powers seemed to have no limits. However they
battled on exchanging blows. Raven blasting larger and larger
holes in the golem and the golem delivering so many powerful
blows that Ravens body began to resemble an amorphous blob
of black flesh holding itself together in the shape of a man.
Within minutes the golem was more wood than earth Tala was

almost out of magic and was getting desperate and that's when she saw it.

Earlier in the fight she had not noticed because she didn't have time to stop and observe the flow of magic, but now Raven was using such a massive amount of power that she couldn't just sense the flow of Ravens magic she could feel it. However that wasn't the amazing thing what she saw was that unlike every other wizard she had seen, Ravens power didn't come from inside it seemed to be flowing into him from the sky from as high up as she could see. Tala's thought to herself "I don't know where your power comes from but if it's not from you than I think I just might be able to win this but I'm gonna need more power"

Tala searched for magic to take in like she had seen her teacher doing when she connected to his power but the land was bare. "Damn I used all the power in the surrounding earth to make the trees there is not a drop left." Suddenly she felt the strong power coming off the golem "The golem! it's pure concentrated nature magic but even with its power I'll still need to use all the power the master left me. It doesn't matter I have no other choice this better work. It's the last trick in the bag" Tala began weaving her spell she collected and channeled all her power to her hand and then siphoned the magic from inside the golem. It continued fighting Raven until she had collected the last drop of its power. Then it collapsed at his feet in a pile of debris. Raven stood confused for a moment then spotted Tala drawing in the last of the power for her spell. He immediately gathered dark energy in a huge ball of power and launched it at Tala but it was too late.

"this is the end Raven" with that Tala unleashed a shock wave of pure earth magic straight at Raven it radiated outward in a green wave swallowing the dark energy ball and reducing it to nothing. The blast continued on to strike Raven, it enveloped him inside and out with a brilliant green light sinking into his every molecule. Raven screamed in agony as he was infused with the power. Raven fell to his knees and slowly the spell faded. Exhausted but unharmed he stood as his remaining wounds healed.

"What, what was that? well it was a pretty light show but it didn't....wait what's happening" again Ravens body began to twist and morph but this time instead of turning into a monster he receded to his normal form .His skin turned back to its normal hue and his wings slowly receded into his back but his face held as he resisted the change. "what have you done to me" I cut you off from the source of your power, its over Raven face it we won" He glared at her his face hot with rage" stop calling me Raven you insolent little witch I'm not that pathetic little whelp , I am a god that weak boy didn't have what it took. So I took his body and rose up to conquer and enslave this land and I will not be stopped by the likes of you and your friends. You may have defeated me for now but mark my words I will return to finish what I started MARK MY WORDS!" and with that the last presence's of darkness disappeared from Ravens face and he collapsed in the dirt. around them the last of the trees burned to the ground and Ravens dark ring of flames dissipated.
Raz stopped just as he was about to exhale a stream of flame on Shorn and let loose an agonized cry "lord Democles no!" The dragon exploded in a blast of black smoke as his summoning magic wore of and he returned to whatever dark land he had been snatched from. Bella stopped mid punch when her opponent suddenly disappeared she transformed back to her human form and looked around for the cause of this sudden change in circumstances. She saw that all the fighting had come to a stop.

"What happened why'd everyone stop fighting?" "I'd say it's because of that" she turned to see Issac injured but alive and

pointing to a spot to the right of her "Issac! are you okay.
..what?" Bella looked in the direction Issac pointed and saw
Raven and Aden on the ground. Tala was leaning over Aden's
body. Issac and Bella ran over to Tala's side Bella gasped when
she saw Aden "is he.....?." Issac examined him "he's alive but
he needs to be healed immediately, Tala can you?" "no" she
spoke without looking away from Aden's body. "I used
everything I had in my last spell, I have nothing left for him. I
tried to heal him before but he wouldn't let me I shouldn't have
listened but he seemed so sure and now…" you could hear the
tears creeping in to her voice as she spoke Issac turned as Shorn
walked up to them "Do you know any healing magic." "I do but
I don't have enough power left I couldn't cast a spell to save my
life. I am truly sorry for my shortcomings" "DON'T WORRY I
CAN HELP" a loud voice boomed Tala jumped up and looked
for the source but she couldn't locate it she turned to ask Issac
about it but he didn't respond, then she noticed.

     Everything was frozen nothing and nobody was moving
or talking. The air in front of her began to shimmer and again
the elven goddess Ælfwynn manifested herself before Tala. She
gasped "mom", "hello Tala It is very good to see you again, and
to see you victorious. You have done very well and to repay
your effort I would be more than glad to help your friend but
first I think it is time we discussed some things don't worry
time is frozen he will be fine while we talk." "We need to
discuss more than a few things first, why did you leave us with
so many questions unanswered in Ælfwynn and without even
telling me what all this is about. Why I am here I've been more
than patient do you have any idea what I've gone few in the last
few weeks." "Yes I have been watching. What has befallen you
is more than you or even I could have ever dreamed could have
happened. It was truly a lifetime's worth of excitement, terror,
adventure, and sorrow. I wonder if I had known how you would

have suffered if I still would have let you come here." "So you did have a hand in me coming here why, why now. Where were you my whole life?" "You have to understand Tala I had no choice I didn't want this life for you but, when the world fell into peril, I knew with the help of the elves you would be able to overcome it and inside you wanted to come too or I would not have been able to bring you"

"Really, I didn't even know about this world, why did it never occur to anyone to tell me before about all of this. What is this world is it even real, and how did you a goddess from another world become my mom. Why am I an elf now is it permanent, can I go home " she let out her stream of questions gasping for air then she let done her shoulders and smiled "huh is it always this fantastic when someone goes crazy" ."I assure you, you are not crazy. You are indeed the daughter of an elf goddess all my children are elves at least in this world and as long as you stay here you will remain one. As for whether you can go home that's a harder question. We gods have rules you see it's why I had to leave in Ælfwynn, it's why you are an elf, and at the moment they prevent you from leaving. These rules may seem unfair but they are meant to protect mortals from us and they did until him." "who?", "the one who caused all of this even the connection between your world and this one the dark god Democles. He did one good thing he created the means for you to come into creation, but he had a child as well. You are all too familiar with him he is Raven.

Against all odds Raven grew up honest and good thanks to Aden and his adopted father. Unfortunately Democles was able to awaken the evil inside him and possess him. It was Democles who you truly fought today and you managed to defeat him and save Raven in the process something even I could not do unfortunately your work is not over. Now listen carefully I would love for nothing more in all of creation than to be able to talk to you further but I have limited time and there are things I must tell you the rest you must find out in time. Democles has not yet been defeated for good. unfortunately we gods cannot harm each other but you can and there are others like you demigods find them. Over the years they have crossed over like you. Working together you will have the power to stop Democles's campaign of evil in its tracks, but be careful he has already sent into motion plans to stop you. The angels carry out the will of the gods on Elysia. As a god Democles had command over our angel forces. It does not surprise me that he used them to destroy Callack, but it mystifies me as to why he had them killed. I'm sure it has to do with those plans and it troubles me deeply. For now go to Nautalias the merfolk city I don't know much but I sense Democles's hand there it is where you'll find the first of the other demigods. I'm sorry that is all I have time to tell you, I've healed your friend you'll need him good luck ,and know I love you and I'm always watching over you."

Tala's mother disappeared as she had come, in a slight shimmer. As time returned to its normal flow everything was exactly as it was before except miraculously Aden's body was completely healed, even his clothes were repaired. Everybody bent over Aden and held their breath. Slowly Aden opened his eyes and looked at them. Tala still absorbing what she had heard from her mother still managed to speak to him first. "Are you alright Aden", "I'm great considering the fact I'm alive means we won." There was a large grin on his face "someone want to help me up." Issac grabbed Aden's arm and hauled him up. "So Tala, tell me what happened" "Well" Tala was interrupted be a rustling behind her as Raven sat up and groaned.

In a flash four swords were at his neck Aden, Issac, Seth and Shorn all ready to stab at the slightest sign of movement,

Aden ready to stab without it. "No wait" Raven shouted. "Give us one reason why" said Aden inching his blade closer to Ravens neck " Aden stop" Tala grabbed Aden' s shoulder urging him to stop "Aden listen to what he has to say." Aden hesitated and Raven took the opportunity to continue "you guys have to listen I'm not the one responsible for this I'm innocent." " Ha! Well that is a bold statement considering not ten minutes ago you were trying to kill us all" Aden interrupted him. "That wasn't me I was possessed by a strong evil I would never willingly do any of this, you know that Aden" Aden stared at him "I thought I knew many things before that day. You claim to have been possessed, what evil influence could have such a hold over you."

"Democles" Tala said the name and all attention turned to her it was silent until Issac broke in "the god impossible." "Is it Issac not weeks ago Tala and I spoke to Ælfwynn herself so is this so unbelievable" Aden started to lower his sword. "It's all starting to make sense the cave…" Aden trailed of and Raven started speaking again "It's all true Aden I never said anything to you or Master Kroft because I didn't want you to worry but I kept secrets from you. Even before he took control I heard his voice telling me what to do and I always refused. He said he was my father and I had to impose his will on Elysia but I didn't listen. I pushed him out for months I resisted but one night his voice was stronger than usual. I couldn't resist he lead me to the temple where he was powerful enough to use our link to take over my body and use it for his evil plans. Master Kroft became his first victim I saw it all but I was trapped and couldn't do anything to stop it he was worried about me and followed me there. Aden I've done unspeakable things under his control I'll understand if you can't forgive me but you need to know the truth" Raven stopped speaking and resigned himself to his fate.

Aden still looked unsure Tala spoke. "he's telling the

truth Aden Ælfwynn told me." Seth spoke up "no matter who was in control a being capable of such evil must die." Issac chimed in "What's to stop Democles from taking control of him again." "when I defeated him I destroyed the link between them." "Tala speaks for Ælfwynn her will is my will" Shorn added to Tala's words. They all seemed unsure Issac finally spoke "who are we kidding we all know this is Aden's decision alone only he can be the one." Seth turned to Aden "Aden you've told me of your hatred for this man are you going to let this murderer live." Aden sighed "no certainly not I swore an oath to avenge master Kroft's death and I will no matter what, so I guess the only question left to ask is how we kill Democles"

Ravens face lit up as Aden dropped his sword and helped him up "it is good to have you back brother" Aden embraced him "you too, it's been a long time" everyone seemed to relax finally swords returned to sheaths and It began to sink in that the battle was over they had won" Tala scanned the battlefield their losses had been heavy but the bulk of the elves and Vel had survived and the werewolves had fared particularly well. the victorious army had already begun to celebrate amongst themselves. The elves prayed silently thanking Ælfwynn for victory while the Vel sang and drunk with some of the more adventurous elves joining in. The werewolves just howled to the sky in victory.

Tala took it all in then turned back to Aden "so what do we do now" Aden let go of Raven and smiled at her "well for now we celebrate with the others , I'd say we earned a break" Tala called the elves over to the Vel camp and that night they had a great festival. Aden brought back Brand good as new in his normal size and he lit a great bonfire. A stage and podium were hastily erected on which Seth was named king. Shorn said some words for those who were lost then Tala got up and spoke to the assembled heroes of Elysia.

"I am young and I don't feel as if I have much of a right to say any of this but I find myself the ruler of a nation so I feel I must. For years the elves have completely secluded themselves from the rest of the country killing outsiders on sight and even before Ravens rise to power tensions were high between our people and the rest of Elysia. This must stop we are all equals here and from now on the borders of Ælfwynn forest will be open to all the people of Elysia. I ask only that you show the amount of respect that or sacred homeland deserves, thank you very much." Tala finished her speech and left the stage.

Aden approached Tala as she descended from the stage "Tala, you always have such inspiring things to say where did you acquire such wisdom." "Oh I just stole most of it from TV." "What's TV", "oh in my world it is an um …. well this is hard to explain its sort of a box and moving images appear on it we watch it for entertainment. "that sounds fascinating you must tell me more later, but back to the matter at hand. Don't you think you should tell them about the situation with Democles they deserve to know" "I agree but you need to tell them this is your world and although I put on a brave face this kind of thing really isn't me, if you knew what a loser I was before I got here you'd probably never talk to me again." "Tala no matter what kind of life you led before you came here. You were the same smart and courageous women I've known you to be. You just needed the opportunity to show it. I would trust you completely to handle anything but you are right it should be me to tell them "

Tala shyly looked away embarrassed by the complement as Aden got on stage and addressed the troops. "No doubt you all have many questions about what went on today particularly regarding Raven. The truth on the subject is probably more than you could imagine and there are a lot of things you need to know I guess I'll start from the beginning" Aden told the whole story of what had happened to him Tala and the truth they had discovered about the true threat that was pulling Ravens strings from the background. He proved to be just as inspiring as Tala his words elegant and strong .He finished his speech with a declaration to search out Democles and bring him to justice his vow brought up a cheer from the crowd. His speech concluded he joined Tala and they walked over to the private commanders camp were Bella, Issac, Shorn, Seth, and Raven were already waiting.

   Tala ran up to Bella and gave her a big hug "I'm so glad you're okay. I was worried about you what happened tell me everything" "well there's not much to tell some of Ravens... I mean Democles's agents kidnapped me and put me in a dungeon at the bottom of the dark castle. Things weren't looking too good for a while but then Issac showed up and he helped me figure out how to use this." Bella showed Tala her moon pendant. "This is a magical amulet apparently at one time they were commonplace it gives werewolves the ability to control their transformation and remain conscious of their actions while transformed. I used it to break me and Issac free. By then the army had left shadow city and was marching for Vel so we easily fought our way out of the castle and hurried here. Along the way we got cornered by a pack of werewolves and I discovered that the pendant had another power. It gives me control over werewolves without a pendant. Once we discovered this I used my enhanced werewolf senses to locate and recruit all the werewolves between Callack and Vel to fight for us in the war against Democles and well you know the rest." "Well I'm just glad you're okay and it's amazing that you don't have to worry about your little wolf problem anymore"

   After Tala and Bella caught up they took a seat around

the fire and joined the others in conversation even though they were absolutely exhausted from battle they were all so happy it was over that they talked all though the night. Aden and Raven talked about their childhoods, Tala told them all about her world, Aden told her more about their world, they discussed plans for the future, and Issac and Shorn offered wisdom to their younger cohorts. That night was the day that they all became friends Raven included. Even given the strange and terrible circumstances that brought him into the group the awkwardness quickly faded due to his friendliness, quick wit, and charm. He reminded Tala a lot of Aden although not quite as rough and tumble. Slowly as dawn approached the conversation dwindled and overcome by exhaustion one by one the heroes excused themselves then went to their tents for some well-deserved rest until only Aden and Tala were left.

  Aden turned to Tala "well it looks like it's back to just the two of us again" Tala smiled and said "so what happens now" Aden sighed "well fist I guess we get things squared away here then we head for the verdant islands that's where we will find Democles and that ally that Ælfwynn spoke of." Tala laughed "that's not exactly what I meant." "well what did you mean" Aden said confused "oh forget it never mind. Hey remember that wizard you fought a little after we first met", "yeah." "Well he wasn't working for Democles and he didn't really even seem evil at all. So who was he it's the only thing that doesn't make sense." "I don't know but I have a feeling we will find out someday" Aden sighed "well I'm gonna go to sleep, how about you." Tala looked at the sun which was just beginning to peak over the horizon "in a minute I want to think for a bit "okay come on Brand" Aden got up and went to his tent and brand lifted off the nearby branch he was perched on and followed him.

  When Aden was out of sight Woodrush who had been

sleeping since the battle and had just woken up tottered over to Tala. She gave him a snack and scratched his chin then stared back at the sunrise and sighed. She was thinking of home of her father she missed them both and hated the fact that more and more she was beginning to feel like home and her old life were nothing but a distant dream or old memory. The worst part of it all was when her mother said she might never get to go home she didn't feel sad she almost felt....happy.

The next few weeks were busy they spent most of their time in Callack but they were constantly going back and forth between Callack, Ælfwynn, and Vel dealing with important matters .Tala had made Shorn leader of the elves in her absence but to them her position was not one that could be passed on and Shorn thought it was important she spend some time at the village. Seth often requested Aden's council on certain matters. After the In Callack Issac had been named the new head minister of the magical academy and Raven had been given his old job in the library. Bella seemed to have gotten over her crush on Aden and had started hanging around Raven. She jumped at the chance to become his assistant. She had also been but in charge of integrating the werewolves into Callack who had been surprised to find when the returned to human form that they were now heroes instead of hated villains.

Soon enough after a few weeks things quieted down and the time for their journey to the verdant islands home of the merpeople had come. Because of the other's duties Tala and Aden where the only ones out of the group able to make the journey but they did not travel alone .Even though they no longer had any contact with the mermen the academy still maintained an ambassador just in case. The ambassador a young wizard no more than a few years Tala and Aden's senior named Turrou would join them we was an experienced water wizard and knew much about the merpeople's culture and customs. He was sure to be of great help to them. They would also be accompanied by a regiment of 5 elite elf warriors. Shorn had insisted on it, Tala had actually talked him down if he had had his way he would have sent half the army.

So They were all packed up and ready to go at the Callack city docks on the Chaunt river, Aden was standing at the end of one of the piers the small boat they were going to be taking was tied there and he was watching their new traveling companions load the last of the supplies onto the boat .Tala walked up to him but he was apparently lost in thought because he didn't notice her approach. "You know Aden you don't have to come I've got these guys with me and my mom said this mission was more for demigods. I'm sure there are more important things you have to do." "Tala I wouldn't miss this for the world I made a vow to stop Raven now I know it is really Democles I have to blame and I will help you stop him. Besides I could never have anything better to do than go with you. We made a promise didn't we?" "I had almost forgotten." "We swore to share each other's burdens and that's what I'm gonna do." Tala looked like she was gonna say something but a voice from the boat interrupted her. "we are ready to set sail whenever you are ready" Aden jumped in the boat as someone untied it from the dock and offered his hand to Tala " you ready" she smiled and took his hand "yes I believe I am"

As Tala and Aden stood at the bow of the craft looking at the upcoming river
she decided she shouldn't feel guilty for not missing home too much and resigned herself to a life in Elysia for the time being .In her heart she knew she would have stayed to stop Democles even if she didn't have to there was a job to be done here after all, she looked over at Aden there where worse places to be.

Epilogue

Turrou walked over to Aden and Tala at the front of the ship "Issac has asked us to take care of a little problem in shadow city first. There's unrest the entire structure or the city has been upended because of the war. Ever since then the city's been in chaos you don't mind the detour do you" "sure, let's do it" said Tala "what's the worst that could happen.

Authors note:

If you have any questions or comments on the book
write an email to

elffireemail@gmail.com

and I will write back to as many as I can.

Also my being able to finish this series and write more
books is related to this one's success so if you enjoy
this book spread the word to family and friends
And leave a positive review

Spell Glossary

(The following glossary of spells was compiled by Tala during her adventures in Elysia. It contains all the spells she has heard spoken. This glossary may serve as a powerful tool for the wizard in training. Unfortunately many of the spells Tala saw were not heard by her, so she could not include them in this glossary.

Bizer- a very small but destructive bolt of fire.

Brace- Sends a powerful shockwave in a 360 degree ring from the user. It is powerful enough to send any close by object weighing up several hundred pounds flying

Flara- a basic spell for summoning fire and bending it to your will. It is very versatile and can be made as powerful as the user wants, limited only by his ability.

Igniskild- envelops the user in a dome of fire that protects the caster

Indirecto— affects the mind of an enemy wizard. It alters their perception and causes them to unconsciously change the target of their spells. It can be used to redirect attacks or even turn them on the caster. A skilled wizard can even use it to alter a person's physical movements

Sennar- enchants an object to attack of its accord. Any type of wizard can learn this spell. However it is extremely difficult to master for even the most experienced and talented wizards shaterra- a stone materializes and is fired at the enemy like a cannonball because of the concentration of power used to make the stone move it requires little energy to perform the spell but it has very significant results

Vatra fasath - sends out tendrils of flame that can burn and physically interact with objects and people.

Velocido- allows the user to run at super speed .The user leaves behind a flaming trail as they run.

Familiars

Phoenix- A large falcon like bird that is constantly aflame. If a phoenix ever dies it can be reborn from ashes. Once a phoenix has bonded with a wizard it will stay with them forever. It is interesting to note that while phoenixes partially consist of fire they are not entirely fireproof. There is a temperature at which they combust.

Golem- A large humanoid creature made from inanimate objects and plant matter. They are extremely powerful and almost impossible to destroy. It takes an extremely powerful wizard to summon a golem and they can only survive as long as the caster wills it. Golems can be made of many different materials depending on where they are summoned.

White hart- A very rare familiar that cannot be summoned. White Harts only appear to worthy heroes to guide them on their journeys. They stay with the hero until the day they are no longer needed then they vanish without a trace. They are different from other familiars in that they do not consider themselves servants of those they are attached to. Instead they fight with them as equals.   Their appearance is similar to giant deer with spectacularly intricate and expansive horns.

Raz- The most powerful familiar that has ever been known to exist. Raz is a dragon an extremely powerful race that are cunning and dangerous. Battling a dragon is a life threatening situation for even the most experienced wizard. Raz is not only a dragon but a dragon king. This makes him the most intelligent and deadly amongst his race the black dragons. Forcing a dragon under your control is almost impossible and requires a god's power.

Made in the USA
Charleston, SC
18 May 2014